W9-CUO-172

Captive
Heart

Darlene Mindrup

Heartsong Presents

A note from the author:
*I love to hear from my readers! You may correspond with me
by writing:*   **Darlene Mindrup**
                 Author Relations
                 PO Box 719
                 Uhrichsville, OH 44683

ISBN 1-58660-166-0

CAPTIVE HEART

Scripture taken from the HOLY BIBLE: NEW INTERNATIONAL VERSION®.
NIV®. Copyright © 1973, 1978, 1984 by International Bible Society.
Used by permission of Zondervan Publishing House.

All of the characters and events in this book are fictitious. Any
resemblance to actual persons, living or dead, or to actual events
is purely coincidental.

Cover illustration by Victoria Lisi & Julius.

PRINTED IN THE U.S.A.

one

A misty rain settled over the smoldering ruins of the once flourishing city of Jerusalem. Roman soldiers plunged their way through the debris looking for anyone trying to hide in the wreckage. Echoing screams could be heard in the distance as more of Titus's troops penetrated the interior of the upper city. The moans and cries of the dead and dying emanated eerily from the burning debris.

Samah huddled against the wall of the women's court where the once grand Temple had been razed to the ground. All around her women, men, and children alike moved, their eyes vacant with the starvation and slaughter of the past several months. Her own stomach ached abominably with lack of sustenance; there had been nothing to eat for some time now. She wondered if her brother had fared any better in the prison.

Lifting her eyes to the night sky, Samah breathed a silent prayer of relief that her parents had been spared witnessing the horrifying event. They had left at the first signs of impending doom. The Lord Jesus himself had warned of the destruction to come before he died. Fortunately, the writers Matthew, Mark, and Luke had included His prophecy among their gospels. As soon as the Christian community had seen the beginning signs, they had fled to the surrounding countryside and beyond.

Her parents had thought that she was safe, also, she and her brother Ramoth. And they would have been, had Ramoth not become entangled in a brawl that left another man dead. Although she had believed Ramoth when he said he didn't do it, the authorities had not.

She couldn't bring herself to leave him while he was still in prison, so she had been caught inside the walls of Jerusalem when Titus had built his siege wall. She tried not to think about the things she had witnessed as a result of the ensuing starvation.

Only moments earlier, she had tried to find out what had happened to her brother, but the burly Roman she had asked had knocked her to the ground and told her to stay put. His eyes had been as glacial as the snow that sometimes fell in the mountains around Samaria.

A young woman crawled to Samah's side and huddled near her. Her whimpering cries of distress touched Samah's young heart. She pulled the young girl close, wrapping her arms around her to share some of her body heat. Both women shivered in silence for some time. Finally, the young girl turned a tear-ravaged face to Samah, her voice hoarse with emotion.

"Why? Why did Jehovah do this to us?"

Although Samah could sympathize with the girl's pain, she had no doubt of the reasons behind it. Even Titus had recognized the destruction for what it was. After he entered the city and saw the massive structures of the towers and walls, his words had fallen with ringing clarity among the defeated citizens.

"We have certainly had God as our assistant in this war, and it was no other than God who ejected the Jews from these fortifications; for what could the hands of men or any machines do towards overthrowing these towers?"

"Jehovah didn't do this to us," Samah told the young girl softly. "We did it to ourselves."

The girl pulled back, her face clearly puzzled. "What do you mean? How did we do this to ourselves?"

"Jehovah gave us everything, even His Son as an atoning sacrifice. The Jews turned their back on the Messiah. Why shouldn't He turn His back on us?"

"The Messiah? What Messiah?"

Praying for guidance, Samah began to tell the girl about Jesus. She had never been reticent about sharing the Good

News with anyone, and now was no exception. Even amid this slaughter, she knew that Jehovah's will would be done. As her story went on, the girl drew farther away, her eyes darkening until they resembled large pools of still water.

"You speak blasphemy," she hissed.

Samah tried to reason with her further, but she sidled away, crawling to the other side of the compound, her baleful eyes resting momentarily on Samah before she turned her face with finality.

Sighing with despair, Samah wondered not for the first time why Jehovah had placed her in this position. Although the pain and hunger were horrendous, she still had no doubts about her Lord's direction. There had to be a reason that she was here. But why hadn't the Lord interceded on Ramoth's behalf? If only her impulsive brother had learned to quell his reckless personality, they would even now be safe in Sychar with their parents. Or were her parents somewhere out there trying to find a way to reach them? Surely they realized that Ramoth and she were still in Jerusalem. The thought only added to her distress, because if her father were caught, he would most likely be sent with others who were destined for the arena in Rome.

Before long Samah's clothes were soaked, and her shivering intensified. Her teeth began to chatter from the decreasing temperatures. Although Jesus had warned that they should pray that this destruction wouldn't come in the winter, the time of the first rains was bad enough.

A sudden swishing sound followed by a thud brought her gaze around in time to see a Roman soldier fall to the ground, an arrow protruding from his neck. There was instant pandemonium as the other soldiers scattered to find protection for themselves as a barrage of arrows fell among those in the compound.

Samah curled into a ball, covering her head with her arms. She began to petition Jehovah in earnest for their safety, hers and that of the others being held prisoner here. The screams of the people being held prisoner drowned out the officers' yells. There was nowhere to hide.

Jerked upwards, Samah felt a large arm wrap around her neck. She was almost lifted from the ground by a Roman soldier using her body as a shield against the flying arrows.

The arrows had been precise. Not a Jew was harmed. Only Roman soldiers lay prostrate in the gathering mud.

Choked by the strangling hold, she pulled ineffectually at the soldier's arm. Other soldiers had taken the opportunity to use women as their shields, also. She could hear the shouts of the soldiers, but she could distinguish no words above the pulse pounding in her ears.

Just when she thought she would faint from lack of oxygen, the soldier holding Samah dropped her to the ground. She slumped into a heap, gathering great gulps of air into her famished lungs.

"Captain!"

At the shout, the man standing over Samah hurried towards another soldier frantically motioning with his arms. They moved quickly toward a small group of soldiers gathered in a semicircle around some object on the ground. Samah could hear their agitated voices even from that distance.

"He's going to *kill* us," one man declared vehemently.

"Fool!" the captain yelled angrily. "Why didn't you shield him?"

"We need to try to get the arrow out," another soldier suggested hesitantly.

"Are you going to try it?" the captain demanded. His look moved around the group. "Any of you?"

Curious in spite of herself, Samah tried to see past their hobnailed boots. Still rubbing her throat, she crawled to the side until she could see what they were discussing. What she saw sent her dark eyebrows winging upward in amazement.

A massive dog lay on the ground, an arrow protruding from his flank. His red-gold fur was matted with blood and mud. Every time a man approached, the dog lifted his head and bared his teeth. He had a mane of fur around his neck that reminded Samah of a lion.

The captain rubbed his hands through his hair in agitation. "Does anyone know where the Tribune is?"

Fearful eyes met fearful eyes, and each man shook his head. Samah was amazed that these arrogant specimens of manhood would tremble at the sight of an injured dog.

"Well, find him, for the love of Poseidon! He'll have our hides if the dog dies."

Several men scurried to do his bidding.

Eyes slowly scanning the perimeter of the compound, the captain barked orders that his men jumped to obey. Before long a young soldier returned with news that caused Samah's heart to sink.

"The assassins are dead, Captain."

"All of them?"

The soldier nodded. "They refused to surrender. We had to kill them."

Sighing, the captain surveyed the occupants of the yard. There was no sympathy whatever in the look he bestowed on the defeated Jews.

"It's what we should do with all of them," he declared harshly before turning and walking away.

"But, Captain," the soldier followed him, "what about the dog?"

A fearful look of uncertainty crossed the captain's face before he shrugged. "Leave him. There's nothing we can do. Only the Tribune can touch him."

"He's not going to be pleased. You know how much he thinks of the animal."

"You have a better idea?" the captain snapped.

Shaking his head, the soldier dropped his gaze to the ground. Samah watched until the others were occupied before she stood slowly and hopped across the ground towards where the dog lay. The animal's sides were heaving, and she knew he must be in great pain.

The fact that she had been born without a foot hadn't stopped her from learning how to walk, but without her crutch, it was so much harder. Wishing she still had her crutch to help her move, she hopped around until she was in front of the animal's face.

The dog stared into her eyes a long moment, his dark eyes glistening with intelligence. Samah knelt beside him. For as long as she could remember, she had had an affinity with animals. They seemed to sense that she meant them no harm, and often her parents had shaken their heads at her menagerie of animals rescued from so many kinds of tribulation.

"Get away from there!"

Several soldiers ran towards her, but Samah held her position. Reaching out, she began to rub her hands over the dog's massive head, talking quietly to soothe him. He allowed her touch, his eyes fixed steadily on her face.

The soldiers stopped beside her, their mouths open in amazement.

"Well, I'm a donkey's udder! How did you do that?"

One man knelt beside Samah and reached for the dog, but he jumped quickly to his feet when the animal pulled back his lips and lunged at his hand. Three pair of eyes fastened on Samah in apprehensive fascination.

She ignored the looks and continued to stroke the dog's head. "It's all right," she cooed. "We only want to help."

Glancing up at the captain, she told him, "I'll hold his head, you break the arrow and pull it free."

One brow rose uncertainly, but he nevertheless moved to obey. His look raked over Samah's emaciated form, and she could tell he didn't have much faith in her ability to hold the animal. She adjusted her position until the dog's head rested on her lap. Continuing to stroke his fur, she nodded for the captain to continue.

Swallowing convulsively, he glanced first at his men and then once more towards Samah. Lowering himself to his haunches, he hesitantly reached out for the arrow. The dog didn't move. Taking a deep breath, he took hold of the arrow and in one quick movement snapped it just below the feathers.

The captain's look flew to the dog, but the animal still lay unmoving under Samah's gliding hands. She nodded her head.

"Go ahead."

The captain motioned to one of his men. "Antony, lift the dog's hindquarters so that I can pull the arrow out."

Nervously, the soldier did as he was told. When the captain jerked the arrow free, the dog yelped, but didn't move his head from Samah's lap. She could hear a collective sigh of relief from those gathered around.

"I need something to bandage his wound," she told them.

One soldier ran to do her bidding and brought back a torn tunic. When Samah had the dog settled to her satisfaction, she glanced up at the captain. "Thank you," she murmured.

He stared at her wordlessly, some nameless emotion passing through his eyes briefly. Turning, he left her sitting there.

Before long another soldier entered the compound, and the captain hastened to his side, snapping a smart salute.

"My name is Fronto," the man explained. "Titus has asked me to decide the fate of the Jews."

"Yes, Sir. I was told that you would be coming."

Fronto dipped his head in acknowledgment. "Any men wearing arms are to be slain on the spot. Those who are too old and those who are infirm are to receive the same."

For a split second, the captain felt pity for the huddling mass of Jews, but only for a second. Remembering friends who had died at their hands, his pity was effectively quashed. His look strayed to where Samah still crouched over the wounded dog. "Too bad they're not important people. At least Titus will make sure his group is kept alive. I don't give much for their chances," he finished, nodding at the group of defeated Jews.

The other soldier's gaze wandered about the quivering group. There was no compassion in his eyes. "We should just kill them now and save ourselves the trouble."

"I suppose," the captain agreed, but there was little enthusiasm in his voice. For him, there had been enough killing for one day.

Samah watched in horror as Fronto walked around the group, swiftly dispatching those who were elderly and weak. At a snap of his fingers, a soldier was ready to strike a lethal blow. There was nowhere to run, and no way to do so. The Jews waited in petrified silence intermittently broken by wails of lament or screeches of fear.

Before long Fronto stood before Samah. Her gaze lifted to his face to encounter his puzzled frown.

"A Jew coddling a dog?"

To the Jews, dogs were anathema. They were scavenging beasts that preyed on other animals and drank the blood of animals and humans alike. It was no wonder the soldier was surprised.

Fronto's look slid over Samah's shrunken form, taking note of the missing appendage. His eyes darkened. "She would be a beauty worthy of the temple of Venus, but I have no use for a cripple." He snapped his fingers and stood back.

A soldier raised his sword, and Samah closed her eyes, waiting for the deathblow. Suddenly, the captain intervened.

"Sir."

Fronto lifted a dark brow in question, awaiting an explanation.

"Are you familiar with Tribune Cassius?"

The lines on Fronto's face deepened with doubt. "I know him well. What has that to do with anything?"

The captain pointed to the dog. "The dog belongs to him."

Fronto jerked his gaze back to the dog in amazement. "Impossible!"

Shrugging massive shoulders, the captain smiled. "Nevertheless, it is so."

Fronto studied both the dog and the girl in silence. His eyes snapped back to the captain. "Explain."

The captain explained everything that had transpired. He

ended by telling Fronto that he had sent word to Tribune Cassius of the dog's injury. Fronto's gaze once more fastened on Samah. She held her breath as she waited for the soldier's verdict. His cold eyes never wavered.

The loud noises receded into the background until nothing remained but the sounds in the courtyard. "Let her live," he finally said. Turning, he walked on.

Samah released the breath from her lungs, thankful to be spared, yet saddened for those who were not.

Suddenly the dog lifted his head from Samah's lap, his pointed ears straining forward. He began to struggle against Samah's restraining grip.

"Easy, boy," she soothed, but the beast refused to be swayed. Struggling to his feet, he stood shaking, his ears cocking to and fro. He stared at Samah, whining. Again, his head jerked upward, and in the next instant, he dragged himself away and disappeared out the gate.

Samah watched him go, feeling as though she had lost her very last friend.

❧

Tribune Cassius made his way among the carnage of the once holy city of Jerusalem and felt a moment's shame. Everywhere death and devastation met his eyes. This once beautiful, thriving city would be no more. Titus had accomplished what he had set out to do. Still, these arrogant, stubborn people refused to bow to the yoke of Roman subjection. Even now, people were being massacred for their open defiance.

Shaking his head, he smiled ruefully. In truth, had they really managed to decimate the Jewish people, or were they now holding a snarling lion by the tail? A more pigheaded lot of people he had yet to meet.

As he drew closer to the Temple, his shame increased. Titus had offered the people the chance to save their monument to their God, but they had refused. Two Jewish zealots were mainly responsible, John and Simon. They had set the Temple on fire after luring Roman soldiers inside. Titus's rage had known no bounds. Both of the miscreants had disappeared, but they couldn't hide for long. Now the once beautiful Temple lay in ruins.

Having left his dog, Sentinel, in the compound where they were storing prisoners, Cassius was now anxious to reclaim him. He had believed the dog would be safer there.

Cassius smiled, thinking of the dog's reproachful glare when he had told him to stay. Sentinel was his constant companion and truly his best friend, having saved his life innumerable times. Cassius trusted very few people, so therefore had very few close friends. Actually, he and Sentinel were a matched pair because Sentinel was as distrusting of people as Cassius was.

The dog had appeared to him one day several years ago. He had been on his way home from a campaign and found the animal sitting next to the road. It was almost as though the dog had been waiting for Cassius to come by, because he had followed him home. Since then, he had been constantly at Cassius's side.

Puckering his lips, Cassius gave a piercing whistle. Those around him stopped and stared, then went on with their business of looting and killing. Cassius tried to ignore them. He continued to stride along, his dark brows drawing down into a frown. Something was wrong. Sentinel should have responded to his whistle by now. Growing more worried, Cassius hurried his steps, once again piercing the air with his shrill whistle.

He was almost to the Temple court when he noticed Sentinel coming slowly towards him, dragging his hindquarters. Alarmed, Cassius ran and crouched next to where the dog had stopped. The animal's panting was labored and uneven, and it was obvious he was in distress.

"Sentinel!" Eyes darkening with anger, Cassius began checking the dog for injuries. When his look lighted upon the bandaged back hip, he frowned even more fiercely. Someone had tended the dog's wound. Several times Sentinel had been wounded before, but no one had been able to come near the dog save Cassius himself. Amazed, he wondered who had managed to do so now.

Gently lifting the dog into his arms, Cassius retraced the dog's steps. When he reached the compound, Captain Sabinus came hurrying towards him.

"Tribune! We have been searching for you."

"How did this happen?" Cassius demanded angrily, ignoring the man's placating tone.

Sabinus swallowed hard. "Assassins, Tribune. But they have all been taken care of."

Cassius glared at the mass of people in the courtyard. "Who tended him? You?"

The captain shook his head. "I only pulled the arrow out. We couldn't get near him, but the girl over there was able to keep him still until we removed it, then she bandaged him."

Cassius's gaze locked on Samah, trying to look inconspicuous among the ragged group of people. Her dark hair hung long and tangled about her shoulders, and her torn tunic showed the lines of her bones from her emaciated form. She lifted large, fearful eyes to meet his gaze, and Cassius felt something clench tightly within his stomach. Though ragged and unkempt, the girl was still a beauty. Pulling his eyes from hers, he noticed the other Jews eyeing her with open hostility, and wondered why.

"Bring her," Cassius commanded.

"Aye, Tribune!" Still, the captain hesitated.

"Well, what is it Man?"

The captain's eyes met his leader's. "She's a cripple, Tribune."

Cassius returned his attention to Samah, and for the first time he noticed her missing foot. He felt a moment's pity that such a beautiful woman should be so afflicted. Shrugging off the feeling, he turned back to the captain. "Then carry her," he commanded brusquely.

The captain hastened to obey. Lifting Samah into his arms, he followed where the Tribune led until they reached a small, empty building being used as a care center. The Tribune disappeared inside carrying his dog. The captain followed.

Cassius motioned for Sabinus to place Samah on a stool next to where he had laid the dog. He watched in surprise as the dog lifted his huge head and gently licked the girl's hand. She, in turn, smiled at the dog and began to stroke his side, cooing softly. Amazed, Cassius fought a primitive surge of pure jealousy that threatened to engulf him.

After a time, the girl's soothing voice affected Cassius as well, and for the first time in days, he felt himself begin to relax. When she finally lifted her gaze to his, there was something dark and secret in her eyes. Though he told himself it meant nothing, his heart suddenly leaped within him at her look.

two

Samah dropped her gaze from the Roman's piercing dark eyes to the panting dog at her side. She felt oddly unsettled, and wondered why. Never before had she had such a feeling, as though her life were about to drastically change in some way—if she had any life left after this night. She knew that things were bound to change anyway, but the feeling persisted that her future had something to do with this bold tribune.

Cassius's eyes held a host of unasked questions, but he focused his attention once again on his dog. His jaw clenched, and Samah swallowed uneasily when he moved close to her side. The leather of his armor creaked as he moved his well-toned muscles. Her insides twisted with terrible fear, and something else she was as yet unaware of.

The air around her was filled with the strong smell of sweat and blood. Though the rain had stopped, the hobnailed boots treading through the small building still splattered mud. Soldiers moved in and out of the small confines of the building, some carrying injured, others seeking audience with the man leaning over the beast. That he was an important leader was obvious.

One young soldier entered and snapped a smart salute, his right fist slamming against his chest. His dark hair curled over his forehead; his helmet was tucked loosely in his left arm.

"Tribune," he spoke rapidly, "I bear a message from General Titus."

Without lifting his inspection from the dog, the tribune snapped back at him. "Then deliver it."

Eyebrows lifted slightly in surprise, the young man's look went from Cassius to the beast lying on the table.

"He requests your presence. He has decided to have a

ceremony honoring all who excelled themselves during the battle."

Cassius sighed, straightening. "When?"

"Tomorrow afternoon. He wants every soldier to be polished and dressed as befits the imperial Roman army."

Cassius knew the reasoning behind this act of the general's. His eyes rested briefly on the bedraggled girl huddled next to Sentinel. No doubt the soldiers would be honored in sight of the defeated and decimated Jews, as another means of demoralizing them. He supposed he should feel remorse of some sort or perhaps pride in the army's achievement, but in reality, he felt nothing. No joy. No sorrow. Nothing.

He motioned to a soldier nearby. "Domitus, spread the word," he told him. "Inform the centurions so that they may inform those under their command."

Domitus and the young soldier snapped simultaneous salutes and quickly exited the room. Their departure left Cassius suddenly alone with his dog and the young Jewish girl. Something about the girl touched a chord deep inside of him. Tumultuous feelings he thought long subdued suddenly reappeared. When Sentinel lifted pain-filled eyes to his, Cassius grew angry all over again, effectively suppressing any unwanted sentiments.

"Your people are stubborn and foolish," he snapped at Samah. "They thought to defy Rome and look where they are now. Slaves. Fodder for the games that Titus is so fond of."

Surprised that he had spoken to her in Aramaic, Samah knew of nothing to say. She refused to look his way, continuing to stroke the sleek fur of the dog that had unwittingly saved her life.

Cassius watched her, feelings of jealousy warring with feelings of gratitude. That she had saved Sentinel was beyond argument, but that the dog had *allowed* her to bothered him greatly.

Samah heard him moving and sensed his closeness. Strong fingers lifted her chin until her frightened eyes met his dark, angry ones. His furious gaze suddenly altered with surprise, and he dropped his hand as though it had been burned.

"You're not a *Jew*!"

Realizing that her eye color had given her away, she turned her look away. "I am from Samaria."

Puzzled, he continued to study her, now thoroughly intrigued. Her eyes were an incredible blue-green, almost the color of the Mare Nostrum, or as the people from these parts would call it, the Great Sea. If she were not a Jew, how had she then been caught in this city, and at a most inopportune time? Perhaps she was a slave and innocent of shed blood. Seeing her state of disarray, the bones showing through her tunic, his mind balked at the thought. One thing he had found out over the past several weeks was that not everyone in this accursed city was guilty of rebellion against Rome.

"And are you a Jew?" He had to know. His war was with bloodthirsty Jews, not unknowing victims.

"No," she told him softly. "My father was a Jew, but he. . . he changed when he married my mother and went to live in Samaria."

"So, you're Samaritans." For a moment he looked nonplused. "How do you come to be in Jerusalem?"

Samah realized that she was on very shaky ground. Right now the Roman's hatred was centered on the Jews, but it wouldn't be any better for her if he knew that she was a Christian. The slaughter of so many of her brothers and sisters by the madman Nero only a few years ago was still very close to her mind.

So much unrest had occurred in the last year since Nero had committed suicide that the Romans hadn't had time or thought to continue their persecution of the Christian sect. The four emperors since—Galba, Otho, Vitellius and Vespasian—had far too many problems of their own.

After the Jews had run the Roman legion out of Palestine and held the territory against the Roman war machine, the hatred of Jews had been fanned into a conflagration. Though

Rome had eventually regained the territory, it had been a bloody battle, and one the Jews had lost sorely.

Realizing that the tribune was awaiting an answer to his question, Samah bit her bottom lip, wondering just what to tell him.

"My. . .my brother and I were here for Passover. We were trapped inside when the zealots closed the gates and refused to allow anyone to leave."

His eyes narrowed to slits. "So, you *are* a Jew."

Samah poured a cup of water with shaking hands and held it beneath the dog's nose. He hesitated briefly, then began to lap thirstily. She turned to answer the tribune's question, but stopped when she noticed his shocked expression. Frowning, she glanced back at the dog, then once again at the soldier, unable to determine the reason for his reaction.

"He has never taken even a morsel from someone other than me."

Cassius came close again and Samah took a hasty step in retreat. She clutched the cup in both hands, her frightened eyes lifted to his. He towered over her slight height, menacing in his uniform that fit snugly across his broad chest. His powerful thighs were visible beneath the short tunic of his outfit, his feet planted firmly apart. He looked every inch the vengeful warrior.

"How have you managed to do this? What form of magic have you used?" Grabbing the cup from her hand, he sniffed it suspiciously. "Have you drugged him?"

Throwing the cup to the floor, Cassius grabbed Samah by the shoulders, pulling her close. His brown eyes glittered menacingly. "So help me, I'll have you whipped within an inch of your life!"

Palms resting against the armor on his chest, Samah let out a small cry of alarm. The tinny taste of fear left her mouth suddenly dry.

"I've done nothing!" she cried. "Please!"

Cassius felt something warm against his forearm, and

glancing down he found Sentinel's mouth gently closed there. The dog whined softly, his sharp eyes seeming to plead with Cassius to let the woman go.

Slowly, he released her, his attention focused on the dog. The dog then loosened his gentle grip and lay back upon the table, his sides heaving with one heartfelt sigh. So shocked was Cassius that he didn't hear anyone else enter the room.

"Tribune."

Snapping his attention back to the doorway, he saw Domitus waiting for his acknowledgment. Still rattled by what had just occurred, Cassius stepped away from the table. "What is it?"

Samah let out her breath slowly. She was certain that the tribune would have more to say on the matter. Although he listened to what the soldier had to say, his look never left her. Truth to tell, she had been as amazed as he was. Though she had always had an affinity with animals, this man's dog seemed to be something out of the ordinary. Had Jehovah truly sent a messenger to protect her and give her hope at a time when she most needed it? Like Balaam and his donkey?

"I have your gear polished and ready for inspection," the soldier told Cassius. "Would you like to check it now?"

Cassius barely heard him. He stood staring into Samah's eyes for what seemed an eternity. Finally, he nodded to the soldier without breaking eye contact with her.

Dropping his look to his dog, he told him, "Stay." Once again, his eyes met Samah's. "I'll be back," he told her softly, and she recognized the subtle threat in his voice.

❦

The sun shone hotly, gleaming off polished armor. Roman ensigns fanned in the cool breeze, fluttering against a bright blue sky.

Cassius awaited his turn to come before General Titus, his mind elsewhere. That Sentinel would turn against him was beyond his comprehension. Though the dog hadn't injured him at all, he had been shocked by the animal's ready defense of the young girl the night before.

He was still trying to puzzle out how a Jew could have such unusual eyes. He knew that she must have mixed blood, and that told him that she was not a true Jew. So exactly why was she in Jerusalem at such a volatile time? She had said something about her father not being Jewish after he married her mother, yet they were still in Jerusalem for their holy Passover. What exactly had she meant by that? How could a Jew suddenly not be a Jew?

She was hiding something from him, he could tell. She had chosen her words with care, heedful not to say something he might find objectionable.

His gaze went to the Jews huddled on the hillsides beyond, unwilling witnesses to the power of the great Roman army. Tightly drilled ranks of soldiers moved as one body, their shining armor reflecting the sun in a brilliant display.

After Titus gave his speech, the air vibrated with the cheers of his men. On and on their shouts of acclamation rose to the sullen captives beyond, fanning their hatred even further. Brooding countenances gave evidence that the sight of the Roman war machine had, indeed, subdued even the most zealous. Had there been any more ideas of vengeance, the sight of so many men in ready defense quelled them.

Again his mind wandered to last night after he had returned to where he had left Sentinel and the woman. He had asked her name, and she had told him. Being fluent in Aramaic and Hebrew, he knew that her name meant *to bring joy*. Since it was obvious that her defect was from birth, he wondered at her parents' giving her such a name.

His own mother had left him on the rocks to die when he was but a babe. Without conceit, he knew that he was without flaw, perfect of form. Why then had his own mother rejected him when this young girl had been given a name of joy? If not for General Anticus, he would have been carrion food. The man had been more than a father to him. What of Samah's father? How had he felt when confronted with a deformed child?

When Cassius's time came, he stepped forward, accepting the congratulations of his general and the golden crown placed on his head. A medallion of gold was hung around his neck.

As Titus stepped back, he smiled. "The loot from this city must be delivered to my father, the emperor, but if there is some small item you wish for your own, make it known to me, and it will be yours."

Suddenly, Samah's face flashed briefly through his mind. He found himself considering an idea that he told himself was utterly ridiculous. He had no need of a woman in his life, and especially one he knew spelled trouble. Still, there was Sentinel to consider.

"Sir, if I might be so bold."

Surprised, Titus nodded for Cassius to continue.

"There is a young woman. A captive."

The look of understanding that passed over Titus's features left Cassius disturbed. The general's slow smile and lecherous look only added to his discomfort. He wasn't certain how to explain his request since he wasn't positive of the reasoning himself.

"She must be quite special for *you* to take notice, my friend. Your hatred for the opposite sex is well known."

Cassius flushed hotly. "My liege," he refuted. "I do not hate the fairer sex, I am merely. . .let us say, careful where they are concerned."

Titus reached out a large hand and squeezed his shoulder briefly. "I understand, Cassius. Take her. The woman is yours."

Placing his palms flat against his thighs, Cassius bowed slightly, then stepped back among his own men.

When he could finally make his way back to the infirmary, he stopped by his own tent and retrieved a small gold disk. Clutching it in his palm, he wondered at his sudden reluctance to present it to Samah. She was but a captive, after all. A slave. Her feelings shouldn't matter to him, but somehow he couldn't get the picture of those liquid blue-green eyes out of his mind.

Growing angry with himself, he slammed into the small building where she awaited him. He had thought that she would be sent with the others when they marched across Palestine, but then he had had that insane idea about keeping her for his own.

It wasn't that he wanted her for himself, but it had occurred to him that she might be just what he needed where Sentinel was concerned. Any time he went to war, he had to take the dog with him because the beast wouldn't eat without him there. It had only taken one such trip to convince him that wherever he went, the dog must go, too. He had returned to a bag of bones, and he promised himself that never again would he let that happen.

The others in the army thought him a lunatic for having such a relationship with an animal, but he couldn't deny the bond that was between them. Only his father had understood. It was through his influence that Sentinel was allowed to travel with him on his journeys.

The others had changed their ideas about him after the dog saved his life countless times. The looks they gave him had changed from ridicule to envy.

Samah glanced up from her position on the floor. One hand was lifted to the table, where she stroked Sentinel's massive head. She quickly scrambled to stand, hindered by her missing appendage.

"Stay where you are," Cassius commanded. Crossing to her side, he lifted the golden trinket over her head, resting the chain against her breast, and for just a moment his breath seemed to weaken. "Keep this on you at all times," he directed her huskily. "It says that you belong to me." Cassius's gaze locked with hers.

Samah pressed her lips tightly together to keep from arguing. She continued to look into his dark eyes, unable to break the contact, her legs seeming to turn to liquid beneath her. He appeared to be probing into her very soul, and she was afraid of what he might see.

A small whine from the table finally caused him to turn away from her. Taking a deep breath, Samah edged away from Cassius while he gave his attention to his dog. Only now was her heart returning to its normal rhythm. Yes, she was afraid of him, but this was something far different than fear.

"I wanted to ask you something," she finally managed to say.

His dark eyebrow curved upwards as he waited for her to continue.

"I. . .I wondered what had happened to the prisoners who were in the prisons."

He turned fully towards her, his eyes narrowing. "Why do you want to know?"

The sullen suspicion in his eyes made her hesitate. "My brother was there," she answered softly. "I would like to know what happened to him."

He smiled without mirth. "Your brother is a very lucky man, then. Titus had all the prisoners released."

Samah's mouth parted in surprise. "But why?"

Cassius shrugged, unwinding the bandage from Sentinel's thigh. "I assume he thought they would be more loyal to him. Since they were mostly political prisoners that your priests had incarcerated, Titus probably felt they were on his side." He glanced back at her. "Why was your brother in prison?"

She found it hard to look at him. "They said he murdered someone."

She had his full attention now. "They?"

"The priests."

"And had he?"

Samah reached for the crutch that she had been given last night. Steadying herself with it, she still refused to look at Cassius.

"He says he didn't."

Cassius leaned his back against the wall, crossing his arms over his chest. "And do you believe him?"

Angry sparks shot from Samah's incensed eyes. "Of course I believe him."

Snorting, Cassius lifted himself away from the wall and came closer. "A sister's love," he derided, his voice edged with sarcasm.

Surprised and defensive, Samah wound her arms around her waist. "I take it you have a sister who doesn't treat you well."

Realizing that he was opening himself up to explanations he wasn't willing to give, Cassius turned back to Sentinel and began to replace the bandage on his flank.

"As far as I know, I have no sisters. Nor brothers either for that matter."

Samah felt instant pity for him. Enemy or no, it must be lonely without a family to care for you. Perhaps that explained his coldness far more than his being a tribune in Rome's army.

"I'm sorry," she told him softly.

Straightening, he turned on her a look filled with wrath. "Save your pity. I don't need it. I don't want it. Better to save your pity for yourself."

Commanding the dog once again to stay, he quickly exited the building.

Samah slid down to the floor, curling down onto the mat that had been her bed the night before. She wrapped her fingers around the gold disk hanging from her neck. For an instant, she was tempted to rip the thing off and fling it from her. Prudence dictated otherwise.

Although her heart was still heavy at being separated from her family, she had one bright spot of hope that her brother was even now on his way home. She prayed that Jehovah would keep him safe and that her family would remain safely in Sychar.

three

When Titus finally withdrew from Jerusalem, he left behind a smoldering mass of rubble. Deciding to leave three of the fortified towers as a testament to his good fortune and to prove that God was on his side, he razed the rest of the city to the ground.

The Phasaelus, Hippicus, and Mariamne towers stood as a lonely testament to the power of Rome as the captives marched from their midst. Other than that, only a portion of the west wall remained to greet those who would try to prove themselves mightier than the Roman war machine. Soon, even the three massive towers would be destroyed, not a stone left on another. The tenth legion that Caesar had left to guard the city stood at attention while the others passed through their ranks.

In his train, Titus led the most beautiful and youngest of the remainder of the Jews. Many had died of starvation, others were sent to the mines in Egypt, and still others were sold as slaves.

Samah realized that she was more fortunate than most. She traveled with Cassius as his personal slave, and though she was looked at with hatred by the other Jews and covetousness by the other soldiers, she maintained her dignity and pride.

She glanced behind her now as the last vestiges of the holy city of Jerusalem disappeared from view. The once beautiful land around the city was nothing more than a wasteland. The soldiers had done their work remarkably well, and the demoralized Jews marched with their heads hung low. Although the Jews greatly outnumbered the Romans, any thought of rebellion had been crushed.

Vultures swarmed the ruins, and it was only as they finally reached a great distance that the smell of blood was once and for all eliminated from the air.

Sentinel walked at her side, head and ears alert. In the past three weeks the dog had had time to heal, and though he walked with a limp, there was no denying that he was ready for action.

Samah wondered again at Jehovah's having used an animal, and a dog at that, to save her life. Since dogs were flesh eaters, the Jews looked upon them with hatred. She marveled again at Jehovah's wonderful love and protection.

Each day she prayed for her family, for the church, and even for Cassius. She knew that everything that happened in life was for Jehovah's glory, and even with a heavy heart at her forced captivity, she knew she would always trust Him.

After three days, the rain began to fall. While soldiers and Jews alike suffered with the cold wetness, Titus ensconced himself in his tent. Though the soldiers had blankets to warm them and food to fill their bellies, the captives did not. Many became ill and died.

Samah stood at the entrance to Cassius's tent and watched the huddled mass of people across the way. She longed to go to them, to offer them comfort, if not with food, then with the words of the Lord Jesus Christ. But she knew she would be rejected. Already many considered her Cassius's concubine. Only a few soldiers knew the truth. Cassius stayed with another tribune and left his tent to her and Sentinel. He chose not to let the others know, for Samah's protection. Why he should be so considerate she didn't know; she just accepted it as another blessing from Jehovah.

She saw Cassius coming towards her now through the misting rain. As always, his handsome form left her feeling slightly breathless. He was indeed a fine representative of what a man should be.

Sentinel got quickly to his feet and met Cassius at the doorway of the tent. Long tail swishing backwards and forwards, he stared in open adoration of his master.

Grinning, Cassius bent to him, rubbing him roughly across

his body. He spoke gently to the dog before turning his attention to Samah.

"You've eaten?"

She shook her head. "No. I was waiting for you to eat first."

Frowning, he rose to his feet. "That's not necessary."

Samah bent her gaze to her fingers twisting the belt on her tunic. "I. . .I wasn't very hungry."

Reaching around to loosen his armor, Cassius lifted a dubious brow. Although Samah had been allowed more food than the others, she was still little more than skin and bones. He dropped his chest piece onto the rug.

"I saw you watching the others," he told her softly.

Her anguished eyes met his. "They have so little, Tribune. Every day more of them die."

His own eyes sparked dangerously. "Well, if you plan on joining them, you can forget it. Bring something for both of us to eat."

Although the army usually traveled with light provisions, having Titus with them had increased the availability of supplies. Samah brought a plate of fruit and bread and placed it before Cassius where he reclined.

"Sit," he commanded, and reluctantly, Samah obeyed.

Sentinel came and curled himself behind Cassius's outstretched legs.

Cassius broke the loaf in half and handed a portion to Samah. She took it from him and nibbled at the crusty edges.

"Samah, many of your people die because of their own stubborn pride. They refuse the portions given to them by Roman hands."

She lifted dark lashes to expose large eyes gilded by grief. "And what of the others? Those who are refused food because they are too old or too sick?"

Cassius shifted uncomfortably, dropping his gaze to the plate in front of him. He took a pomegranate and rubbed it on the side of his tunic. He handed it to Samah and then took another for himself.

"There isn't enough food for all the captives," he told her roughly. "It needs to be given to those certain to survive."

Cassius realized his words sounded hollow even to his own ears. Growing angry, he threw the pomegranate back to the plate and sat up. "Enough of this discussion."

Samah remained silent as he got up and restlessly wandered around the tent. He looked at her over his shoulder. Something in his eyes set her heart to pounding. For three weeks she had been in his presence almost every day, and each day saw her fear of him decrease to be replaced by a growing attraction. She wasn't certain which she feared most.

"Tell me about yourself."

Dropping her look away from his, she lifted one shoulder. "What would you like to know?" she asked, and he didn't miss the hesitancy in her voice.

Sentinel crawled to her side from where he had been lying, and Samah gave the dog what was left of her piece of bread.

Seeing her reluctance, Cassius's eyes narrowed. He came back to where she sat and seated himself across from her. The intensity of his look unnerved Samah. She had never been reticent about sharing her story with anyone, but the fact that the man across from her represented all the power of Rome made her hesitate. Romans hated Christians, of that she was certain. But perhaps it was for this very reason that Jehovah had brought her to this position. She would be careful with what she said, but she would be honest.

"I'm a Christian, Tribune."

His eyes widened in amazement. He said nothing for some time, and Samah could see him trying to digest what she had revealed and how it would affect him.

"I'm surprised that you would admit it," he told her finally. "Surely you know that that religion has been forbidden by the emperor."

Samah smiled slightly. "Which emperor? I know of Nero, but I have heard nothing of Vespasian's thoughts on the matter."

"Then let me apprize you of his feelings," he told her dryly.

"Should you happen to mention it to him he will most likely have you burned, if not crucified."

She opened her mouth, but the words dried up in her throat when he reached across the space between them, cupping her chin in his palm. His eyes were dark with anger.

"You will say nothing of this to anyone; do I make myself clear?"

Although she knew that the apostle Paul had said that one must obey one's master, she also knew that he had said to obey God above all else. She finally managed to push the words out of her mouth.

"I will not lie."

She saw his eyes darken further. "You will if I command you to."

It took every ounce of strength she possessed to shake her head negatively. She was more than a little frightened by his rigid stance. His nostrils flared outwards, and he released her.

"If you are foolish enough to admit to such a religion, I will not protect you."

Cassius looked at her and was mesmerized by the dark promise in her eyes.

"You won't have to, Tribune. If Jehovah is for me, who can be against me?"

"Rome," he ground out savagely.

The word shivered through Samah, bringing pictures of the last few months. Indeed, Rome was a powerful enemy, but even the power of Rome had not been able to silence the words of the mighty Jehovah and His Son. Though Rome had tried to stamp out Christianity, the opposition had only caused it to grow. If not for the great persecutions by the Romans, the word would never have spread to the outermost reaches of the empire and beyond.

Paul gave his life, as did Peter and James. As for the other apostles, no one was certain what had happened to them. Only the great John was left. But if the apostles could give their lives, she could do no less. The problem was, she wasn't certain that she had their strength.

Cassius leaned back upon his outstretched palms, fixing Samah with a steely look. "And your parents? Are they Christians, too?"

Though she had little fear for herself, she wasn't about to betray her parents.

"Your silence tells me what I need to know."

Samah felt her stomach clutch with fear. She lifted frightened eyes to the Tribune's face.

"We are truly harmless, Tribune."

He laughed harshly, leaning forward and pinning Samah with a glare. "Harmless? I watched a friend executed because he refused to recant such a foul religion. He was a good soldier, but he was taken in by your false beliefs."

"Not false," she refuted resolutely. "There is only one God, and He sent His Son to die for the atonement of the world."

Getting to his knees, Cassius reached forward, grabbing Samah by the shoulders and pulled her face close to his. "You will never speak such atheistic nonsense again! Do you hear me?"

Cassius heard a low whine behind him, but he was undaunted. Turning his head, he snapped at Sentinel. "Go. Lay down."

The dog refused to budge, though he made no other move towards them. Cassius turned his attention back to Samah.

"You will remain silent on this issue. That's an order."

Samah knew there was no use arguing with him. He had worked himself into a fine state of wrath. Dropping her gaze to the floor, she allowed him to think that she had agreed.

He slowly released her. Getting to his feet, he looked from Sentinel back to her. Leaving his armor where it lay, he ducked out of the tent and disappeared from view.

❧

The journey across the desert was long and arduous. At every province, Titus stopped and took time to relax. He used many of the captives to provide entertainment, and many of them were forced to kill one another or be thrown to the wild beasts. Cassius was careful to keep Samah away from the vicinity of these entertainments, but the rumors of them spread around the camp.

For every person that died, Samah felt her guilt grow. She should share the love of Christ with them before they died. They should know that the Messiah had already come and that He had atoned for their lives. Even if they rejected her message, at least she would have delivered it. Yet Cassius's command hung heavily on her mind, and she had to admit, she was afraid.

The longer they traveled, the more wan Samah became. It was hard marching hour after hour using a crutch. Even now a sore had been rubbed under her arm, but she tried to ignore it. Regardless of her own troubles, she could see that she was far better off than the others.

Finally, Titus decided to hole up and winter in Caesarea. To keep boredom at bay, the games continued.

After a time, Samah could stand it no longer. She knelt on the ground one night and lifted her face to the star-spangled heavens. "Oh, Lord. I know they rejected You, but haven't they had enough?" Her voice was ragged with despair. "There will be no more of Your promised people left."

Words seemed to echo through her mind. Words that she had heard long ago among the congregation of believers. Words the Lord Jesus had told to His disciples.

Whoever does the will of my Father in heaven is my brother and sister and mother.

Jehovah's people. The ones who do the will of the Father. The Jews had been chosen to be Jehovah's special people, to bring into the world His only begotten Son, but they rejected Him. Time and time again she knew that to be true. Her own father had been persecuted by his own uncle, as had her own Uncle Adonijah. Together, they had gone to Samaria, a land hated by the traditional Jews, and taught others about the love of Jesus.

She loved to hear the story of how her grandfather's sister had met Christ at Jacob's well. He had turned her life around with just a few words of acceptance.

"Samah."

Jerked from her thoughts, Samah clumsily stood. Cassius faced her across the way, his face shadowed by the light coming from the tent behind him.

"Come inside," he ordered.

Samah followed him into the tent. One look at his stony face and she could see that he was seething.

"I gave you a command."

Biting her bottom lip, Samah held out her hands placatingly. "I have not disobeyed your command."

"I saw you praying just now," he argued.

"You did not command me not to pray."

For just a moment he looked confounded. A muscle twitched at the side of his mouth.

"Then let me clarify my order. You are to have nothing to do with this. . .this *Christian* religion."

Samah watched him warily. Every time she saw him in all his Roman paraphernalia, it frightened her. Should he so choose, he could give her as the next victim in Titus's gruesome games. Shivering, she still tried to answer him boldly.

"Being a Christian is what I *am*. It's not something that I *do*."

Cassius crossed to her, his hands clenching and unclenching at his sides. He saw her eyes widen in fear. She should be afraid. He wanted to take her and shake her into submission. Never before had he encountered such stubborn resistance, especially from a mere girl.

He was sorely tempted to find a way to make her submit, if not by force, then by guile. She was a challenge to him, and he had never been able to back away from a challenge.

But could he do it? Pictures of those who called themselves Christians floated through his mind. Nothing, not even the fangs of a wild animal, had been able to make them recant.

What could he possibly do to ensure Samah's obedience? He decided to change his tactics. Reaching out, he gently pushed her long, dark hair behind her ears. The clean, silky texture tempted him to slide his fingers through it. Giving in to the temptation, he did so. Something flashed briefly through her eyes, and Cassius didn't miss it. He took advantage of it, moving even closer.

Cupping her face between his palms, he told her softly, "Then *be* a Christian, but do not *do* it."

It was hard to think with him so near, but she understood his message. He didn't want her to show her faith before others, but since it was such an integral part of her life, how could she not? She didn't know what to say to relieve his mind of worry about her life, because she could tell that he was truly concerned about her. But her life was in Jehovah's hands.

"Tribune, I cannot deny who I am."

He took a deep breath, releasing her at the same time. Head reared back, his voice became biting. "Then a new command I give to you. Do not leave this tent again."

Samah felt her heart drop to her toes. Every day she looked forward to walking about outside. Though she was careful to stay within sight of their camp, the fresh fall air was invigorating just to breathe.

"What of Sentinel?"

It had fallen to Samah to take Sentinel for his daily exercise, and both looked forward to the time spent away from the camp. Samah might have feared for her own safety were it not for the huge beast walking protectively by her side.

"He'll come with me."

The words held finality. Samah hung her head, but kept her mouth closed on the arguments she wanted to put forth. She wanted not only to tell others about the love of Jehovah's Son, but she wanted to share it with this man, also. It had become so important to her that she had burst forth with her proclamation of Christianity without a thought.

She feared Cassius, but not that he might cause her harm. She feared only the strange reaction she seemed to have to his presence.

She looked up only when she heard him leave. Sinking slowly to the floor, she began to pray.

༈

When she saw Cassius again the next day, he seemed preoccupied. He commanded Sentinel to stay in the tent with her and left.

Later, he came into the tent and began to collect his gear.

"Titus has agreed to allow us to leave for Rome. My father is ill."

"Your father?"

He lifted an eyebrow, smiling slightly. "I do have one."

Frankly, the thought had never occurred to her. He handed her the rug she used to sleep on. "Get ready to leave. I've booked passage on a cargo ship leaving this afternoon. The sea might be kind of rough this time of year, but I have no choice."

In a way, Samah's prayers had been answered. She wouldn't have to witness any more Jews dying at Titus's hands, but this was not exactly what she had meant by her petitions.

Cassius stretched his arms over his head, the muscles of his chest tightening his tunic. "It will be good to be home."

Samah wasn't so certain. She had heard numerous stories of the corrupt city of Rome. The sun was briefly hidden by a cloud, and Samah felt a chill pass through her at the darkness. It was almost as though that darkness had passed right through to her soul.

It finally penetrated her mind that she was about to leave her homeland, the land of her birth. Except for trips to Jerusalem, she had never been outside her own vicinity of Sychar. Now, she might never see her family again. The darkness seemed to increase.

Cassius noticed her sudden stillness. He dropped his arms slowly to his side, brows drawn together. "What's wrong?"

The gathering tears in her eyes brought a sudden lump to his throat. He walked across and bent to look into her face.

"Samah?"

"My family," she whispered brokenly.

He looked at her with understanding, his lips parting slowly. It only now struck him that she was still but a child, a child who was about to be torn from her way of life. For the first time in his life, it bothered him to see a woman upset. Never before had he given any thought to a woman and her tears. He didn't know what to say.

Noticing her distress, Sentinel came and nudged his muzzle into Samah's hand. He whined softly, seeming to understand her dilemma.

Cassius felt like something that had crawled from the swamps. He looked from one to the other and, for a moment, was tempted to leave them both here. Realizing the foolishness of that thought, he turned away and began to gather their supplies.

"I'll leave the packing to you. I must take my leave of Titus."

Samah watched him leave the tent and wondered what kind of life she would lead in Rome. She had heard so many stories, and when she was younger she had wanted to visit that city. But then there had been Nero, and she had decided that such a ruler didn't speak well for the populace of the city.

How could a people be so ignorant of the one great God and fear Him so much that they would destroy His people? Whatever had happened to Roman tolerance? And whatever was going to happen to her?

four

The hulking cargo ship creaked and groaned, sliding into the dock on the Tiber River with practiced ease. The city of Rome stretched before Samah's astonished eyes, the clay-tiled roofs spreading as far as the eye could see.

The gangplank was dropped, and men moved quickly up it to the deck of the ship. Within moments, the whole ship was alive with activity. A stuppator nimbly scooted down the scaffolding hanging to the sides of the dock and expertly began to caulk the ship.

"What do you think of it?"

Samah tensed at the unexpected intrusion. Cassius moved close behind her, his eyes roving the bustling port. That he was pleased to be home was evident in the proud timbre of his voice.

"It's very large."

How inadequate, thought Samah. Nothing had prepared her for the magnificence that lay before her astonished eyes. Even the great Jerusalem paled in comparison, and she had always believed it to be the grandest city on the earth.

Cassius smiled slightly, cocking his head downward to see her face. "Much more imposing than Jerusalem, isn't it?" he inquired, as though he had read her thoughts.

Samah nodded, but remained silent. Rome was indeed more impressive than Jerusalem, but Jerusalem had something that Rome did not. It had the almighty Jehovah. At least it had until His people turned their backs on Him and rejected His precious Son.

"Truth to tell, even in the great Rome, there is not much that can compare with the Temple Herod built in Jerusalem." His breath gently stirred the hair on Samah's cheek, and her hands clenched the ship's rail.

"The Temple that is no more," Samah contradicted softly.

Cassius sighed. "You are correct in saying so. It was a pity that it had to be destroyed."

There was genuine regret in his voice. Samah turned her head slightly and found his face very close to hers. The growth on his chin gave him a rugged look that was oddly attractive. When her eyes met his, she saw something flash briefly through them, his look focusing momentarily on her lips. Her own eyes grew large, and she tried to move away from him, but the ship's bulwark dug into her stomach, letting her know that she had nowhere to go. Sensing her tension, Cassius instantly moved from behind her to her side, his look once again focused on the city beyond.

"What will your people do now without their Temple?"

Samah's face softened, and she looked to the azure blue sky. "God no longer lives in temples built by man."

Puzzled, Cassius lifted a questioning brow. "Then where does your God live now?"

"In our hearts." Samah answered him so softly that he had to bend to hear her.

Snorting, Cassius turned, leaning his back against the ship's bulwark. "The priests'?"

Samah shook her head, suddenly reluctant to continue with the conversation. She glanced at him again, and realized that he expected an answer.

"No. God lives in the hearts of everyone who has accepted Jesus as Lord."

"And Jesus is?"

"God's Son."

Sudden comprehension filled his features. "Ah, yes. I remember now. Your Christian religion."

Samah wanted to say more but didn't think now was the time. Already she could tell the tribune's attention was on something else. Turning, he looked across the deck, his lips tilting into a small smile.

"Sentinel has never done well on the water."

Samah followed his look and felt her heart go out to the poor beast. The dog's eyes were filled with pure abject misery, his massive head lying on his outstretched front paws. It was hard to imagine a more pitiful sight.

Cassius reached to his feet, lifting the pack lying there, and the dog's head instantly came up, eyes and ears alert. Cassius chuckled softly.

"Come, Boy. It's time for us to go home."

Lunging to his feet, Sentinel quickly reached their side, his huge tail moving back and forth. Cassius took Samah by the arm and led her to the wooden plank that reached to the dock. Struggling with her crutch, Samah felt her insides twist with sudden fear. She had to tell herself over and over again that Jehovah was with her no matter where she went. As she had told the tribune, He dwelt in her heart. This thought brought a measure of peace, and she was able to follow Cassius through the streets of Rome with a small amount of equanimity.

Although Cassius was not in uniform, it became obvious that he was well known by the many soldiers who saluted him along the way. Often he stopped to share a word with one of them. Their interest in her was obvious, but he declined to explain her presence. He kept his conversations brief.

When he reached the market, Cassius slowed his steps. He turned to Samah.

"Are you hungry?"

Surprised that he would consider her, Samah quietly agreed that she was. Nodding briefly, Cassius turned back to the shops around him.

"Let's see. What can we get?"

He bypassed the tavern, knowing that it would be extremely crowded at this time of day. Since most of the poorer families had no kitchens of their own, they chose instead to get their meals at the local tavern.

The crowd mingled around them, the noise level increasing with each passing minute. Samah watched the people haggling at the vendor's stalls, adding their purchases to already heaping baskets that they carried. It didn't take her long to realize that most of those doing the carrying were slaves. It seemed that even the poorest people owned slaves of their own.

Several musicians played their instruments, their trumpets, tambourines, and lyres adding to the already surging din. People dropped coins into the small baskets at their feet. When Cassius passed them, they smiled hopefully at him. Digging a coin from his pouch, he dropped it in with the others. For some reason, this gave Samah an oddly warm feeling.

A long queue of men waited near a Roman with a basket of wheat. At Samah's interested look, Cassius explained, "Those men have no jobs. The government gives them free wheat to support themselves and their families."

Samah remembered the times that fellow Christians gave to a communal pool so that other Christians who were in want would not go without. Brothers and sisters cared for each other as Jesus had commanded. In doing for others, Jesus had said that they were doing also for Him. Having the government do so relieved the people of that obligation. She regretted that this was so, for the people missed out on one of Jehovah's true blessings. The difference was, one was done by taxing the people severely, the other was done in love.

Cassius stopped beside a fruit vendor's table. "How about a pomegranate?" he asked, lifting one up for inspection.

The bright fruit made Samah's mouth water. She nodded her acceptance. Handing her the fruit, Cassius took one for himself, giving the shopkeeper the required coin.

Cassius polished his on his sleeve before taking a huge bite. The juice dribbled down his chin, and he wiped it away. There was laughter in his eyes when he looked at Samah delicately pecking at her fruit, but he said nothing.

Samah thanked the vendor for the fruit, and he quickly glanced at her in surprise. He continued to study her periodically, albeit surreptitiously. She could feel his regard, and wondered at his continued interest.

Cassius's attention was suddenly caught by a ruckus across the street. He frowned.

"Wait here." His command was brusque, and obviously meant for both her and Sentinel. Both watched him cross the street and become embroiled in an angry conversation with two other citizens.

Though the dog kept his attention riveted on Cassius, Samah turned back to study the vast array of colorful fruits on the counter, some she had never seen before. The vendor obligingly told her their names and what countries they originated in. He smiled at Samah, and she found herself returning his smile. There was something soothing about the young man, and his courtesy went beyond the bounds of vendor propriety. It wasn't forced, but was actually an integral part of him.

He seemed to be studying Samah as thoroughly as she had studied his fruit. Growing uncomfortable under his perusal, she dropped her gaze.

"Pardon me," he spoke softly, "but you don't seem to be from these parts."

Samah lifted her look to his face and found him intently watching her.

"I'm not," she responded unwillingly

He swallowed hard, his throat moving up and down in agitation. He glanced quickly around him before lowering his voice. "If it would not offend you for me to say so," he suggested hesitantly, "you sound like someone from Judea."

The simple words had a profound effect on her, and one the vendor hadn't expected. The sudden shock of the bold statement left Samah feeling suddenly lightheaded, the world reeling giddily around her. Placing a hand to her forehead, she tried to bring her world back into focus. Obviously the long travel and periods of fasting, mixed with the oppressive odors of Rome, were having an effect on her.

The vendor hurried out from behind his counter. "Are you all right?"

Samah stared at him blankly. Frowning, he hastily searched

around him, finding a basket and turning it over.

"Here. Sit here."

He reached to help Samah sit on the upturned basket, but a low rumble from Sentinel brought him suddenly upright. Glancing hesitantly at the dog, he warily bent until his face was even with Samah's.

"My name is Jonah. If there is anything I can do. . .?"

He left the question hanging. Placing a hand on Sentinel's bristling fur, Samah lifted suddenly bright eyes to the young man's.

"Jonah. A Jewish name."

A light seemed to fill the young man's face. "Yes. I am Jewish."

Wondering what the young man's reaction would be, Samah lifted honest eyes to his.

"I am from Samaria."

Jonah smiled. "I thought as much. Your eyes are a dead giveaway."

Surprised, Samah stared at him wordlessly. Most Jews hated Samaritans with a passion. She had lived with such prejudice most of her life. Only among the Christian believers had she found the freedom to be accepted for who she was.

"Samah. What's wrong?"

So engrossed had Samah been in her conversation with the young Jew that she had failed to hear Cassius arrive. He glared suspiciously from Jonah to Samah.

She stood unsteadily, swaying slightly. Cassius reached out and took her by the arm, his eyes darkened with worry. He made a tisking sound with his tongue.

"I should have realized. You'll never make it to the villa in this condition. It's too far." He stood, lips pressed between thumb and forefinger, pondering his dilemma. "I can't get you a cart until the sun goes down, nor a chariot for that matter."

Jonah stared wordlessly from one to the other. Noticing Samah watching him, he quickly looked away.

Cassius addressed himself to Jonah. "Is it all right with you if she stays here until I can arrange for a litter?"

Jonah looked surprised. "Of course."

Cassius turned his look back to Samah. "Wait here. I'll return shortly." His narrowed gaze went slowly over Jonah from head to toe. He pressed his lips together tightly. "Sentinel will keep you safe." The words seemed more of a warning for the young vendor.

Three pair of eyes watched him vanish among the crowd. Jonah glanced at Samah and then at Sentinel still watching where his master had disappeared.

"Please, sit down."

Samah did so, her legs already wobbling beneath her. Jonah returned to his position behind the counter. Whereas he had been friendly before, he was now reserved. Samah wondered at his sudden reticence. Though she tried to engage him in conversation, his answers were brief and curt. Aggravated, she finally stopped trying and concentrated instead on the sights and scenes around her.

Several people came to Jonah's stall to purchase fruit. His attitude was always the same, regardless of the person's position. He treated everyone with gentle courtesy. Obviously he was well liked by the people, for his stall was never empty for long.

Trying to stay out of the way, Samah began to search the area around her, hoping that Cassius would return soon. When Jonah reached to remove a cluster of grapes hanging above, Samah noticed the symbol carved onto the post of the stall. The fish emblem had been hidden by the cluster of grapes, but now was very evident.

Sucking in a breath, she stood quickly. Jonah's look followed hers, and he jerked his gaze back to hers, his face going deathly white. Samah was thankful that there were no customers.

"You're a Christian!"

If anything, Jonah's face paled further at Samah's breathless declaration. His eyes were wide with fear, his lips opening and closing silently.

Samah's joyous eyes met Jonah's frightened ones. "Praise Jehovah! You're a Christian!"

Jonah's shoulders slumped with relief. He glanced about him and moved closer to where Samah sat. Leaning over the counter, he lowered his voice.

"I thought you were a Christian! Somehow I just knew."

"But why didn't you say something?"

Jonah's face colored hotly, and he quickly looked away. "The Roman you were with. . ."

Samah understood his confusion. Placing her hand on his where it rested on the counter, she told him, "I am his slave. We have just arrived from Jerusalem."

He stared at her in shock. "Jerusalem?" he whispered in horror. "You were there for the destruction of Jerusalem?"

Thoughts of the horrors she had witnessed were reflected in her eyes. Samah nodded solemnly.

His eyes clouded with pity. "We have heard rumors. Is it true that the Temple was destroyed?"

Samah nodded again. "Just as the Lord foretold."

Another customer briefly took Jonah's attention. Samah watched him, marveling that he was a brother in Christ. Hadn't she known her Lord wouldn't forsake her? She had heard of fellow believers in this city but thought they had all been eliminated by Nero years ago, and others since.

She saw Jonah hand the customer her purchase, smiling in return. It suddenly occurred to her that Jonah was without a beard. He wore instead the mark of the Romans with their clean-shaven faces and short hair.

Seeing his handsome face, she wondered why her people chose to hide their features behind a face full of hair. What would her brother and father look like without their beards? Would they be as handsome? She thought probably so, for both were fine of form. Jonah's strong chin was visible, even when he was smiling.

He came back to her now. "Would you like to meet with the others?"

Samah smiled with delight. "There are more believers here?"

Jonah returned her smile. "Oh, yes. Not as many as there were before." His face darkened briefly. "But there are still quite a few of us."

"I would love to!" The bright hope slowly ebbed from her eyes. "But I don't know where you meet, and I don't know what my life will entail. I don't know if I will be allowed that freedom."

He nodded in sympathy. He opened his mouth to speak but stopped when Sentinel let out a loud woof. Cassius was striding in their direction, closely followed by a small litter being carried by four slaves.

He pulled up in front of them, his look going briefly from one to the other. Narrowing his eyes at the sudden tense atmosphere, Cassius took Samah by the hand.

"Come."

He helped her into the litter, then turned his gaze back to Jonah. They studied each other a moment before Jonah finally turned away. Cassius clicked his fingers to Sentinel, and they once again started on their way. Neither one noticed when Jonah nodded to a young boy across the street. The boy lifted himself from the wall where he had been reclining and slowly ambled in their wake.

Samah felt foolish being carried along like some rich ruler. She hunkered down behind the drapes, embarrassed to be in such a position. It had been this way for the past several days.

On the ship she had tried to assume her role as slave, only to be blocked at every opportunity by Cassius. He never allowed her to be anything important, but he was equally unwilling to allow her to be a slave. His attitude confused her.

One moment he would be kindness itself, gentle and protecting; the next he would be cold, and though not harsh, decidedly aloof. Now here she was riding along like a patrician while Cassius strolled at her side like some plebeian. It left her unsettled, feeling as though she had no real part in this world to which she had been taken.

"The fruit vendor seemed quite friendly."

His voice came to her from outside the litter, and something in it warned her of his displeasure.

"Not overly so," she assured him. "He merely passed the time with me until you arrived."

She could hear his grunt. "And what did you find to talk about?"

Samah wondered at the suspicion in his voice. "Mostly his fruit. Some of it I have never seen before." Pushing back the drapes, she looked out at him.

Cassius could see the confusion in her face. He wondered himself at his attitude. There was something in the young fruit vendor's eyes that left him wanting to strangle him with his bare hands. These strange emotions left him feeling as though he were out of control, something he had never experienced before. Sometimes the feeling made him so angry that he lashed out at Samah, only he knew she was innocent of the cause. Still, he had never had these feelings until she had entered his life.

They walked in silence for some time, Samah noting with interest the many things surrounding her. It was only as they drew abreast of the arena that her face paled and she pulled her head back inside. Horrifying images of brutally murdered Christians passed through her mind, leaving her cold and shaken. She didn't look out again until the litter drew to a stop.

Cassius helped her alight and turned to the slaves. "You may return to your master."

Samah watched them go. "They aren't yours?"

Cassius chuckled. "No. I don't have slaves and litters stored all over Rome for my eventual use." He grinned down at her. "They belong to my friend Andronicus. His house is near the market where we stopped."

He handed her the crutch, noting the weary lines in her face.

"You're tired. Come inside."

She followed him up marbled stairs, past great columns and through the entrance. They entered the atrium, the waning afternoon light still filtering through the opened roof. An upper balcony surrounded the upper story leading to rooms beyond.

A servant met them by a small pool, used to catch rainwater, directly below the atrium's roof. He was an older man, his gray hair sprinkled with only a few touches of brown. His portly belly jiggled when he walked, but it was his eyes that caught Samah's attention. They were a bright blue and aglow with happiness.

"Master," he said. "It is good to have you home."

It surprised Samah that he actually seemed to mean it. Cassius smiled.

"Hello, Democritus. It's good to be home. Come, let me introduce you to someone."

Democritus's eyes fixed curiously on Samah.

"Democritus, this is Samah. She is now a member of this household." Quickly veiling the shock in his eyes, Democritus offered a tentative smile. He awaited further instructions, obviously confused by his master's declaration.

When Cassius next spoke, there was no denying the authority in his voice. "She has but one job, and that is to care for Sentinel."

Democritus's appalled look flew to the dog standing placidly at his master's side.

"If she can be of assistance to you around the house, so be it, but you are *never* to take her from her duties of caring for the dog. Am I understood?"

Democritus nodded, nonplused. Though things might have been far from clear to him, he would never have thought to argue the point.

"Take her and see that she visits the baths." Samah's face turned crimson under both men's regard. "And find her more suitable clothing. I'll leave that to you, but I want to see some color."

Samah didn't think she could be any more embarrassed. She was wrong.

"Oh, and find her a room close to mine."

Samah's eyes went wide, but Cassius ignored her. Democritus's knowing look rested on her briefly.

"And send word that I wish to see Justinian."

"The carpenter?"

"Yes," Cassius agreed. "The carpenter."

Cassius glanced down at Sentinel, patiently waiting. He rubbed the dog briefly, smiling as the beast squirmed and whined under the attention. Straightening, he pointed to Samah.

"Protect."

With that, he turned and exited the villa, leaving Samah and Democritus staring open-mouthed after him.

five

Cassius entered his father's villa with some trepidation. The missive he had received had stated very little except that his father was in critical condition. His sandals tapped against the cold marble tiles as he moved through the atrium that was a much larger replica of his own.

He felt his insides twist at the mere thought of losing the man who had raised him as his own son. Only months before General Anticus had found Cassius on the rocks, his wife had died in childbirth along with her babe, and Anticus had brought Cassius home and showered on him all the love he would have given his own child.

Later, for some reason, the general had felt it necessary to tell Cassius of his true origins. Cassius wondered if his life would have been different if he hadn't. Perhaps he wouldn't have this intense hatred of women, and he would have married and settled down by now. And then again, perhaps hatred was too strong a word. Mistrust would be more apropos. Still, the thought brought him no comfort, no feelings of anticipation to share his life with a woman.

Hector, his father's personal servant, showed Cassius into the triclinium, where he found his father lying on a couch pondering the view of the gardens from the opened doors. He took a moment to study the older man without being noticed. Though he had lost weight, he still held his shoulders erect. Cassius felt himself relax slightly. He wasn't certain what he had expected, but he had definitely expected something much worse.

"Hello, Father."

The general started, turning abruptly to face Cassius. Joy instantly filled his face.

"Cassius! By the gods!"

When the older man tried to struggle to his feet, Cassius became concerned. Hurrying to his side, he gently laid a restraining hand on his father's chest.

"Don't bother to get up."

His father eased back against his couch. Searching for signs of ill health, Cassius slowly seated himself on the couch opposite the general. Although Anticus's face was wan, Cassius felt some measure of relief at the vitality glowing from his dark brown eyes.

"It's been a long time," Anticus told his son. "This campaign was a lengthy one and in a most wretched place."

Cassius nodded. "I couldn't agree with you more. It's good to be home."

Anticus motioned to the platter on the table at his side. "Something to eat, Cassius?" The old man's eyes roved his son's dusty figure, noting the growth of beard on his face. "You came straight here?"

Cassius held up his hand in rejection of the food. "I wanted to see for myself how you were."

The general's keen eyes missed nothing in their slow perusal. "You look tired, my son." He chuckled. "And dirty."

Cassius's lips twitched. "Somehow I thought that cleanliness was not quite as important as seeing for myself that you are well."

Warmed by his concern, Anticus smiled. "Well, as you can see, I am fine."

That was not the whole truth, but Anticus thought it best not to burden his son at this time. He knew his son well enough to know that something of import had happened in his life, but he also knew it was best to allow Cassius to share whatever it was at his own leisure.

"Can you stay for the evening meal?" he asked.

Relaxing back against the couch, Cassius breathed out softly. "I'd like that."

"Good, good." Clanging the gong on the table, Anticus

addressed himself once again to his son. "Why don't you make use of my bath while they prepare the meal? Relax. Take your time. We will have plenty of occasion to fill each other in on the past years."

When Hector entered the room, Cassius rose to his feet. "I'll take you up on that suggestion. I feel like I have a year's worth of Palestinian dirt on me."

Anticus laughed. "You look it, also." He turned to the servant. "Hector, take Cassius to the bath and make certain that he's given a clean tunic."

Hector bowed. "Yes, my lord." Although Cassius knew the house well, Hector motioned him forward. "This way, my lord."

Cassius followed the servant down the hallway that led to the back of the house where his father had his private bath. His mind wandered to the years he had spent running among the corridors here. Though he had never had a mother's love, he had had a good childhood, safe and secure in his father's love.

Why his father had chosen to tell Cassius about his mother he didn't know, but from that moment on there had been an angry burning in his heart that he could never find solace for. Though he had taken his pleasure with women from time to time, he had never given his heart to any one of them.

A picture of Samah's innocent face flashed through his mind, and for the first time in his life he felt a twinge of guilt for his past offenses against the women of his acquaintance. Being unattainable had seemed to only make him more in demand, and he had taken full advantage of the situation. It had also given him great pleasure to walk away from a brief relationship with his heart intact. The same could not be said of the women. At the time, he had enjoyed the thought of inflicting pain, but now he felt a slight twinge of regret that he had chosen such a path.

"I will send Crastus to you, my lord, when you are through."

Pulled from his thoughts, Cassius nodded slightly and began undressing. The warm water did indeed look inviting.

"Thank you, Hector. A good massage will feel nice after such a long journey."

Sliding into the water, Cassius lay back, relishing the silky warmth of the water sliding over his skin. A low growl of content emanated from his throat as he ducked beneath the water, gratified to be once again in his father's home with others to care for his needs. Though he had faithful servants of his own, none had been with him as long as Hector and Crastus.

When he finally rose from the pool, Crastus was waiting. Wrapping a towel around his waist, Cassius moved to the table and lay down on it.

Grinning up at the giant Philistine, Cassius warned him, "Don't be gentle, my friend."

Returning his grin, the masseuse took an amphora of oil in his hand and removed the stopper. "You needn't worry, my lord. The last thing a soldier needs after battle is *gentleness.*"

Crastus began rubbing the oil over Cassius's body, massaging as he went. The pounding and kneading soon relaxed Cassius's overworked muscles.

"Crastus, how well is my father, really?"

The servant found nothing odd in the young master's question. Crastus had been with the general since before Cassius was brought into their family, and though he was in truth nothing more than a servant, he was closer to the general than anyone, save Cassius himself.

The big man shrugged, continuing his rubbing. "It would be best for you to ask the master himself."

Cassius turned slightly until he could see Crastus's features. There was no duplicity in the servant's face.

"You know he will try to keep me from worrying." Cassius snorted softly. "Imagine if I were commanding a regiment and the general kept information from me to keep me from worrying about how many foes I had to battle."

Crastus grinned, lifting the strigil from the table. He began to scrape the oil from Cassius's skin. "I think the analogy hardly applies," he disputed.

"Doesn't it? The one thing having complete information does for you is to help you prepare for what's to come."

Their eyes met, and Crastus was the first to look away. He pulled another towel from the rack and began to pat Cassius with it. When their eyes met again, Cassius could see resignation in the old servant.

"The physician says that the master has only a short time to live. I didn't understand all the particulars, but the master did."

Cassius felt himself go cold all over. He quickly sat up, grabbing his tunic. Throwing it over his head, he jumped from the table and headed for the door.

He found his father still reclining in the triclinium, the table beside him now set for the evening meal. He motioned for Cassius to take the couch opposite him.

"Have a seat, Cassius." Noticing the set look of his son's face and the fact that he hadn't yet shaved, he sighed. Obviously Crastus had shared something he shouldn't have. "Let's eat before you launch your attack."

Aggravated, Cassius pressed his lips tightly together to keep from bombarding his father with the questions he held tightly in check. Taking his cue from Anticus, Cassius kept up a steady flow of small talk while they ate, though his stomach churned with anxiety. He regaled his father with tales of his journey through Palestine, but other questions burned on his lips.

"I heard you had been lifted to rank of commander," his father beamed proudly. Cassius nodded, his mind on other things.

Anticus wiped his hands on the cloth provided and threw it on the tray. "I also heard rumors of Titus distributing his wealth among the troops?"

It was more a question than a statement. Cassius pursed his lips, wiping his hands, also.

"Not quite, but he did reward those who excelled."

Anticus lifted his goblet towards Cassius. "And of course, that included you."

Cassius watched his father drink his wine, wondering what

the old man would say when he informed him of the reward he had received. Lifting his own goblet, he swallowed a large gulp of the cold liquid, hoping to dislodge the lump that had formed in his throat.

"I was rewarded, yes."

Anticus heard the hesitation in his son's voice. Lowering his goblet, he studied Cassius's face. The look there sent the old man's eyebrows flying upwards. He waited for Cassius to continue.

Taking a deep breath, Cassius met the full force of his father's probing brown gaze.

"I received a woman. It was all I asked for."

Anticus stared at his son and didn't know what to say. At the declaration, his own wits had scattered to the four corners of the earth. Cassius asking for a woman? He stared at his son as though he had suddenly sprouted two heads.

"This woman. She was Jewish?"

"She's a Samaritan."

Anticus's eyebrows rose to his balding pate. "Is there a difference?"

"Not really." Cassius stood and paced to the window overlooking the garden. "And then again, yes, I suppose."

Totally confused, Anticus didn't know what to ask next. He was saved from having to make that decision when Cassius turned back to him.

"Sentinel was injured."

Wondering if his son was trying to change the subject, Anticus shrugged, though there was concern in his voice. "He is well?"

Cassius nodded. "Now. Thanks to the woman."

Anticus slowly leaned back against the couch. "Perhaps it would save time if you just explained."

So Cassius did, leaving out nothing, not even the fact that Samah was a Christian.

Anticus's eyes narrowed. "A Christian, you say?" He pressed his lower lip between his thumb and forefinger, a habit his son had long since formed. "That's very interesting. And where is this woman now?"

"At my villa."

"I would like to meet her."

The softness of Anticus's voice was belied by the intensity of his regard. Cassius wondered at the fixed look on his father's face.

"I will bring her tomorrow," he told his father. Coming back across the room, he smiled down at Anticus. "Which reminds me. I have business to attend to at home."

Anticus rose from the couch despite Cassius's remonstrances. He waved away his son's offer of help.

"I will look forward to your visit tomorrow. General Trajan will be coming in the afternoon. Perhaps you could come then."

Cassius smiled. It would be good to see his adopted uncle. "I'll do that."

At the end of the walkway, Cassius looked back. His father barely had time to adjust his face into a smiling mask, but Cassius had missed nothing. His father was in pain. Extreme pain. How was it that he had gotten so sidetracked from the inquiries he had been so determined to make? His father had always had the ability to twist a situation to his own advantage, and now Cassius realized that Anticus had done just that. Well, tomorrow he would not find it so easy. Tomorrow he would have his answers.

Samah stroked Sentinel on his head, rubbing her hands against his ears. The dog leaned into her hand. Regardless of what people told her to the contrary, she could swear the beast was smiling.

She seated herself on the edge of the small pool beneath the roof's opening. Leaning over, she trailed her fingers in the cool water. She could see her reflection and marveled at the change in herself.

Her dark hair hung in a flowing mass down her back, dropping across one shoulder while she continued to gaze into the water. The soft yellow tunic clung to her figure, giving her more the shape of a nubile young woman than an emaciated slave. Although her figure could not be considered as yet fulsome, she had filled out more in the last few weeks supping at Cassius's table than in the past few years. Frowning at the thought, she realized that she was less than pleased with the idea.

Glancing down at her bare foot, her gaze skimmed briefly over where her other foot should have been. Not for the first time in her life, she wished she were completely whole. Sighing, she smiled at the dog.

"You don't care that I'm missing a foot, do you? Would that all people everywhere had such blindness where faults are concerned."

Sentinel whined, coming to instant attention when he heard a sound at the front door. When it opened to allow Cassius to enter, the dog was beside his master in an instant. Samah noticed the wagging tail and realized that she was just as happy to see Cassius. There was absolutely no reason she should be, but the feeling was there nonetheless.

Cassius glanced at her briefly, and then again, much longer. He straightened slowly, taking in her changed appearance. A sudden veil seemed to shutter his face. Before he could say anything, Democritus entered the room.

"Welcome home, my lord." His eyes briefly scanned Cassius. "I see you made use of your father's bath. Shall I tell Argon that you won't be needing him?"

"Please do. Has Justinian arrived yet?"

"No, master. He sent word that he could not make it until later this evening."

Cassius nodded, going to the doorway that led into another room. "When he arrives, send him to me here." He glanced at Samah. "Come with me."

Lifting herself with her crutch, Samah followed him into the room, gasping at the beautiful murals painted on the walls. The room was lavishly furnished, with statues of various gods littered about it. She quickly turned her face away, but not before Cassius noticed.

He sat on a couch and indolently reclined back among the cushions. "You disapprove?"

Samah didn't know what to say. She felt Cassius watching her, and turning, she found her gaze captured by his. When his eyes slowly traveled over her, she felt her stomach constrict in alarm. Why she should suddenly feel threatened she couldn't understand. If Cassius had wanted to take advantage of her, he had already had plenty of opportunity to do so. Still, her body grew rigid under his careful inspection.

Democritus entered the room, dispelling some of the tension. He handed Cassius a marble box inlaid with petals of gold. After he left the room, Cassius lifted the lid.

"Come here." His soft command brought back all the fear Samah had been trying to keep at bay. Hesitating, she saw his brow rise once again. He awaited her compliance, and she could tell that he wondered what she was thinking.

Taking her courage into hand, she crossed to his side and stood looking down at him. His dark-eyed gaze was void of any emotion.

"Sit here."

Following his pointing finger, Samah dropped gracefully to the floor before him. He lifted a golden bracelet from the box and reached for her arm. It was in that instant that she recognized the jewelry for what it was. A slave bracelet.

He fastened it upon her upper arm, his warm fingers staying wrapped just below the band.

"It says that you belong to me." The oddly possessive note in his voice sent the fear cascading through her once more. "No one will bother you now. The band has my insignia upon it."

He released her, watching the relief she couldn't disguise. She bowed her head, awaiting further instructions.

"Have you eaten?"

The abrupt question brought Samah's head jerking upwards. She shook her head slightly. "I believe Democritus wasn't quite certain what to do with me," she told him ruefully.

Cassius smiled wryly. "Probably not. There has never been a woman servant in my home."

Surprised, Samah could only stare. A host of questions passed through her mind, but she knew it was not her place to ask them. She lowered her gaze to the floor, still waiting for Cassius to make his wishes known to her.

He leaned forward suddenly, lifting her chin with his hand. When his eyes met hers, she was caught by the fierceness of his look.

"Do you miss Palestine?"

Her eyes searched his for the reasoning behind his question. Did he really care what she felt?

"Yes," she answered softly. "I miss my family most of all." Remembering the fruit vendor's words, she thought about the Christian family waiting for her here in Rome. She had only to find them. The thought quieted her escalating fear.

Cassius allowed his fingers to trail down her throat, watching the panic return to her so expressive eyes. He turned away from her, banging the gong next to him.

When Democritus answered his summons, he told his servant to take Samah and give her something to eat. Surprised, the Greek exchanged looks with Samah.

"Come with me."

Cassius halted them at the door. "When she is finished, return her here. Justinian should be here by then."

Bowing, Democritus led Samah away. She followed him along the corridors until they reached the kitchen. A residue of smoke still hung in the air from the preparation of an earlier meal. Since there was no ventilation other than the door, it would take hours for all the smoke to dissipate from the room.

Samah seated herself at the wooden table, watching Democritus confer with the cook. Both men looked at her, the cook's eyes gliding over Samah in an offensive manner.

"You say she is a servant here now?" His look fastened on the slave bracelet.

Democritus shrugged. "I'm not quite certain what her role is. But the master said give her something to eat, and I wouldn't do it sparingly."

The cook didn't miss the subtle warning. He nodded briefly. "As you wish."

Democritus left the room, and a heavy silence fell. Samah could sense the cook's dislike of her and wondered what she had done to cause it. Lifting innocent eyes to his face, she asked him outright.

Seemingly surprised at her forthrightness, he looked nonplused for a moment. Bringing a tin bowl of fruit, he dropped it on the table in front of her. Glaring down at her, he shrugged his shoulders and turned away.

Samah refused to be daunted by his snub. She picked at the grapes, watching the cook as he cleaned his kitchen. He glanced at her briefly but quickly turned away.

"My name is Samah."

Manners dictated a reply to the brief statement. Taking a clay pot from a shelf on the wall, the cook answered her gruffly.

"Cleopas."

Emboldened by this brief success, Samah finished the fruit in the bowl and brought the container to Cleopas. "Is there some way I can help?" she asked quietly.

Cleopas looked at her a moment, his gaze softening slightly. "No. Democritus said that you are to return to the master."

Samah nodded, turning to the door. "Thank you for the food," she told him politely and saw his eyebrows lift a fraction. He said nothing when she left the room.

After following her way back through the hallway, Samah stood hesitating in the atrium. Should she just walk into the other room, or should she wait until she was summoned? It occurred to her that she should have waited for Democritus's return.

As though in answer to a summons, Democritus appeared beside her.

"Come."

Samah waited until he knocked on the door and received permission to enter before going past him into the room. She stood just inside the doorway, noticing that another man had joined Cassius. He must be the carpenter Cassius had summoned. Not knowing what else to do, Samah stood frozen to the spot.

Cassius glanced up at her. "Come here."

Having used a crutch all of her life, Samah moved with uncommon grace across the room.

"Justinian, this is the woman I was talking to you about."

The carpenter looked at Samah with pity. She pulled back in surprise when Justinian moved to kneel before her. Glancing at Cassius in alarm, she calmed slightly when he told her, "Be still and allow Justinian to see your leg."

Disconcerted, Samah stood quietly while Justinian lifted her tunic to see her leg. She was surprised when he pulled a wax tablet from his pouch, and using a stylus to write, he jotted down notes to himself.

Cassius was watching Samah. "Do you think you can do it, Justinian?"

The carpenter got to his feet. "It will be a challenge, but, yes, I think I can do it."

Samah looked from one to the other, still embarrassed.

Cassius handed the carpenter a coin. "Let me know when you are finished, and I will see that you receive your full payment."

Justinian bowed slightly. "Thank you, my lord."

After he left, Cassius came to stand beside Samah. He looked down at her and smiled, a smile that did funny things to her insides.

"Hopefully, you will be able to walk without a crutch before long."

Mouth parted in surprise, Samah tried to read his expression. What exactly did he mean by that?

"And then," he said smoothly, "we will talk of repayment."

six

Samah followed Cassius through his father's house, Sentinel traipsing at her heels. Cassius stopped suddenly in the doorway leading to the peristyle, and curious to see what had stopped him, she moved to the side until she could see around him.

Anticus stood leaning heavily against the stone fountain in the center of the garden, his right hand clutching his toga against his chest. Pain lined his features, leaving him looking gray and drawn. Glancing at Cassius, she saw his mouth turn down into a frown.

"Father," he called softly.

Startled, the older man whirled to face them.

"Cassius." He looked disconcerted for a moment, but quickly composed his features. "Come in. Come in."

Cassius refused to be deterred any longer. His questions *would* be answered. He opened his mouth to say so, when his father suddenly looked past him and smiled.

"You must be Samah," he said, holding out his hand towards her.

Samah responded to Anticus's gentle courtesy like a flower responding to the sun. Her own returning smile reflected her feelings. Moving past Cassius, she took the outstretched hand offered her.

"Welcome, my dear," Anticus greeted, pulling Samah forward and seating her on the bench next to the fountain. He took the seat beside her, his dark eyes studying her face. When Sentinel took his place near her, a look of surprise crossed the older man's face.

Cassius stood watching the scene with mixed feelings. What was there about this woman that could so instantly bring someone under her spell? In truth, he had thought of seeking out a soothsayer to see if by divination the woman was truly some kind of witch. The things he had heard about Christians left him little doubt that there was something odd in these people.

He worried about Samah's continued influence over Sentinel. Would she one day be able to make the dog attack and perhaps kill him? And for that matter, what about his own feelings where the woman was concerned? He was beginning to look for reasons to be near her, and when he was away from her, she so often intruded into his thoughts that he was distracted from his work.

Anticus looked up. "Come join us, Cassius."

Cassius crossed to them, seating himself on the edge of the fountain. Lifting a dry flower petal from the ground, he began to crumple it into a thousand pieces, trying to think of some way to broach the subject closest to his heart.

"Father, you are not well." Cassius's voice was rough with his feelings. He didn't know what else to say, what else to ask.

"Crastus told you, no doubt," his father agreed heavily.

"Only. . .only that you have so little time." Cassius went down on one knee before his father. Anxiety radiated from his dark eyes, so like the older man's looking back at him.

Anticus took his son's hand between his two smaller ones. His concerned face mirrored his son's love.

"Cassius, we all have to die some time. I have had a good life, the best that a man could have. That a man could have two chances at happiness in the same lifetime is beyond comprehension. Both my wife, Drusilla, and you have made that possible." His voice grew ragged. "I have been truly blessed."

Samah felt a lump come to her throat. Seeing the love between the two men left her yearning for her own family. Her heart ached with the longing to be held in her father's arms again, to feel her mother's gentle goodnight kiss. It had been over three years since the beginning siege of Jerusalem, and she had been trapped in the city without her family. Save

Ramoth. And he had been arrested soon after their arrival.

"We'll get you the finest physicians available," Cassius told him sharply. "I have never been that impressed with Phlegon."

Anticus smiled sadly. "Nothing will change the will of God."

Surprised, Cassius looked up. "Which god?"

Anticus looked at his son, a closed expression coming over his face. He turned away from Cassius's probing gaze.

"Cassius, regardless of incantations or potions, I am going to die. I have accepted that. Now you must, also."

Cassius got to his feet, angrily brushing a hand back through his hair. "I refuse to accept that." His voice grew scathing. "And you should, also. One of Rome's finest giving up without even a fight!"

Samah watched the two men warily. Though Anticus was not Cassius's true father, it didn't show in their attitudes. Both were stubborn to a fault.

She caught Anticus's eye, and frowned. There was a look in his eyes that left her feeling suddenly defenseless.

"Cassius," he said, "why don't you find Hector for me. I sent him to Castor's house next door."

Cassius frowned, glancing from his father to Samah. That his father wanted him out of the way went without saying, but he refused to go quietly.

"Send one of the servants," he argued stubbornly.

"They are busy," Anticus answered smoothly. His pleading eyes lifted to his son's. Sighing with resignation, Cassius strode from the garden, Sentinel trotting after him.

Anticus waited until his son was out of earshot before turning to Samah.

"Cassius tells me that you are a Christian."

There was something in his voice that caused Samah's heart to start pounding. This man was a general of Rome. Though he was retired, he obviously still held much power. Yet, there was something about him.

"I am," she agreed softly.

His eyes lit with laughter. "Of all the ways to answer my

prayers, that God would choose to do it this way!"

Confused, Samah hesitantly asked, "To which god are you referring?"

His smile broadened. "Why to *our* God of course. The one you call Jehovah. The one and only *true* God."

Samah sat staring at him in stunned amazement. "Are you a God-fearer?" she asked, referring to the name given to proselyte Gentiles who chose to be Jewish without obeying the Jewish dictates of diet and circumcision.

"No, no, my dear!" He took her hand, squeezing slightly. 'I am a Christian."

Samah's mind was numb. "I. . .I don't understand. Cassius. . ." Her voice trailed off.

Anticus's lips pressed tightly together. "My son doesn't yet know. I found the truth while he was away in Palestine." His eyes took on a faraway look. "Strange, isn't it, how I found the Savior when my son went to destroy His people." He smiled at her again. "And God sent you to me just when I needed you. Oh, how I have prayed for Him to send someone to teach my son about Jesus."

Samah struggled to stand, pulling her crutch up with her. She couldn't sit still. She moved away from Anticus and stood staring down into the rippling flow of the fountain. The sound of the water spewing from the fish's mouth to the pool beneath was oddly soothing.

"I still don't understand." She looked back at Anticus, her brows drawing down into a frown. "Why can't you tell him yourself?"

He got up quickly and came to her. "Oh, I can, and I will." Sadly, he lifted his hand and allowed the flowing water to tumble over his outstretched fingers. "But there may not be time."

He stroked his wet fingers down her cheek. "That's where you come in, my dear. Surely God sent you just for that purpose. Why else would Sentinel be so drawn to you if not by the will of God?"

Suddenly frightened, Samah returned to the bench. Was it

possible that Jehovah would use a common dog to do His will? She had wondered such before, but to hear Anticus say so clearly what she had suspected herself was like having her thoughts made solid. She leaned her crutch against the fountain next to her and turned to Anticus.

"Surely he will listen to his father. I have seen the love between you," she told him seriously.

Anticus joined her. "Sometimes, love is not enough."

Their conversation ceased as Cassius returned to the garden, followed closely by Hector.

"You wished my presence, my lord?"

"Yes, Hector. I need some gall to mix with my wine."

Cassius's head snapped around. "You are in pain?"

Taking a deep breath, Anticus smiled reassuringly. "It comes, and it goes." He looked at Hector. "You know where it is, Hector."

"Yes, my lord."

After he hurried from the garden, an oppressive silence hung in the air. Anticus turned to his son. "Now don't look at me like that. I know what you're going to say, and you might as well forget it."

Cassius's dark look warned of a brewing temper. "Did anyone ever tell you that you are a very stubborn man?"

Anticus waved his hand airily. "Many times," he agreed complacently. "Now let's go inside and have a seat. I have something very important to tell you."

"Father," Cassius complained irritably. "Just tell me."

Cassius saw his father's one eyebrow lift slightly, and he sighed. He knew that look. His father was determined to have his way. Well, let him, as long as Cassius could get to the bottom of this situation.

Sentinel's ears lifted when Anticus reached to help Samah stand, but he remained quietly by Cassius's side. Even though Cassius had had Sentinel for some years, the dog refused to give his trust to Anticus. It could be said that he just tolerated the older man.

Cassius followed his father, who allowed Samah to precede him. He was burning with curiosity over what his parent had had to say to his slave.

They seated themselves in the triclinium, where the servants were busily laying out the evening meal. Anticus motioned for Samah to take a seat, and then he sat beside her on the same couch. It was normal to eat reclining on the couches instead of sitting, but then, Cassius realized, his father had never been a very normal person.

The other servants noticed Samah's slave bracelet and flashed a look at Anticus. He shook his head slightly, frowning at them. Cassius's eyebrows lifted slightly. Whatever was going on here now? Something had changed about his father in the last three years since he had been away. There was an unusual bond between his father and the servants.

It was clear that Anticus had no intention of discussing anything until after the meal. He had always been that way, believing that sour conversation would cause a sour stomach. Cassius resigned himself to a longer wait. He watched in silence as his father drank the brew of bitter gall and wine to help dull his pain.

Anticus addressed himself to Samah.

"Tell me about yourself, my dear. You are Samaritan, Cassius tells me."

Samah's troubled look fixed on Cassius. She was uncertain just how much he would want her to divulge. "I am from Samaria. In actuality, Samaritanism is a religion much like Judaism. There are some minor differences of philosophy, but they still believe in the one Jehovah."

"And has Christianity reached into Samaria?"

Cassius leaned back against his couch, his narrow-eyed gaze fixed steadily on his father's face. "You have a surprising interest in Christianity."

Anticus seemed to steel himself before turning to his son. "That's because I am one."

The quiet words brought Cassius up off the couch, his body

tense, his eyes flashing fire. "By the gods! You've got to be out of your mind! I knew there was something odd going on here! Do you know what you're saying?"

"Sit down, Cassius." The command in Anticus's voice brooked no denial.

Samah watched father and son glare at each other, both pairs of shoulders set uncompromisingly. She swallowed hard, offering a prayer for guidance on Anticus's part.

Cassius was the first to relent. Slowly, he seated himself on the couch, his food now forgotten. He glared at Samah as though it were all her fault. She said nothing, but Anticus didn't miss the look. He laughed.

"You needn't glare at Samah like that. She had nothing to do with it. If you want to blame anyone, blame Trajan."

Shocked, Cassius looked at his father. "Uncle Trajan? What has he to do with this?"

Anticus sighed. " I had hoped to wait until Trajan was here to speak for himself, but I can see that you won't wait."

"You can say that again!" Cassius lifted a peach from the platter and then threw it back again. He glared at his father. "I can't believe this!"

"And you needn't look at me as though I had suddenly become demented," Anticus ground out.

Cassius flushed. That had been his exact thoughts.

Anticus's voice softened. "Cassius, there are things that I need to say before. . .before it's too late."

Cassius felt the anger drain from him. This man was his father and the only person he had ever loved with unconditional devotion. Nothing could change that now. There was something on his father's mind that he wanted to disclose before he died, and Cassius would just have to bear with it. A tight band seemed to close around his heart.

"Go ahead," he told his father. "I'll say nothing until you are finished."

Nodding his head, Anticus glanced once at Samah and then started to speak.

"I need to start at the beginning. When you were born."

Seeing the brief spasm of pain that flashed across his son's face, Anticus hesitated. Gathering his courage, he finally continued.

"Your mother didn't leave you on the rocks to die."

Cassius's eyes widened, his face going suddenly pale. Forgetting his earlier promise, he interrupted. "What are you saying?" he croaked hoarsely.

"It was not your mother who left you on the rocks to die, Cassius. It was her husband."

Cassius could hardly breathe. "My father? How long have you known this?"

Though his voice was steady, the reluctance in Anticus's voice couldn't be missed. "I've always known."

A sudden surge of billowing dark anger boiled up in Cassius. His body began to shake with barely controlled fury. "Go on, don't stop now," he commanded snidely. "So my father was the one to disown me."

Sighing, Anticus continued. "Your father was not your mother's husband."

The silence in the room was almost deafening. Anticus's voice seemed unusually loud when he continued. "Your mother was in love with a young legionnaire. She and her husband had an arranged marriage, and her husband was very brutal to her. Needless to say, she found solace and comfort in the arms of a soldier in Florian's regiment."

"Her husband is a soldier?" Cassius interrupted again.

The look Anticus gave Cassius was hard to interpret. "He was. He died some years ago."

"And my mother?"

"Your mother was the friend of my sister. I grew to love her as much as I loved your Aunt Penelope, so when she needed help, I was there for her." Anticus took a knife from the tray and began to pull the skin from a peach, not so much to satisfy his hunger as for something to do. "She became pregnant while her husband was away on a campaign. She was frightened of the consequences if he should find out it was another man's child, as well she should have been. He eventually did find out, and he almost killed her. After you were born, he snuck you away one night and left you outside the city to die. The rest you know."

Samah could see Cassius struggling to understand everything Anticus had just told him. She wanted to reach out to him. Comfort him. She wanted to give him the kind of love he had never known from any woman. Realizing her thoughts, her own mind was thrown into sudden confusion.

Somewhere along the way over the past several weeks, she had begun to care about the Tribune Cassius. Frightened, she turned away lest he could see her feelings registered in her eyes.

"Where is my mother now?" Cassius rasped.

"I don't know," Anticus answered heavily. "I kept track of her until just before you left for Palestine, then suddenly she disappeared. I have had men searching for her for some time."

"Did she know about me?" The pain in Cassius's voice brought tears to his father's eyes.

"Yes. She expected Florian to do something, so she had a servant always watching him. He followed Florian outside the city gates and then brought you to me. She asked me to take you in as my own, and I was more than happy to do so."

"Why did she never come to see me?"

Anticus sighed. "Florian would have killed you. She loved you enough to make that sacrifice. Then by the time Florian had died, you were already my son. She didn't want to change that."

"Why didn't you tell me this before?" Cassius couldn't bring himself to look into his father's face.

"I promised that I wouldn't," Anticus told him regretfully.

"Then why now?"

Anticus scooted forward on his seat until he was close enough to touch Cassius. He laid his hand gently against Cassius's rough one.

"Cassius," be began quietly. "I am a Christian. I knew that when you returned to Rome I would have to tell you the truth. I cannot go to my grave with a lie in my heart. To God, lying is an abomination."

"God," Cassius spat. "That's something I will have to take up with Uncle Trajan."

After that one declaration, silence permeated the room for some time. Finally, Cassius turned to his father. "I need some air."

"Cassius. . ."

"Please!" Cassius grated. "I need time to think."

Anticus regarded him steadily. "As you wish. But you will come back, won't you? Trajan will be here soon."

Cassius snorted. "Something else I need to think about."

"My son. . ."

"Father, I love you. Let's say no more right now."

Cassius turned to Samah, his look inscrutable. "Stay here. I'm sure you and my father have much to talk about."

Flinching at the caustic tone of voice, Samah lowered her head in obeisance.

Snapping his fingers, Cassius called to Sentinel. "Come on, my friend. I feel like having your company."

Feeling snubbed, Samah watched them leave the room.

"He'll be all right," Anticus soothed. "I'm certain of that now."

"Now?" Samah questioned, her brow knitting in confusion.

Anticus smiled. "Why, now that you are here, of course."

"My lord," Samah said disbelievingly, "I think you credit me with too much."

Handing her a section of grapes, Anticus told her, "Have faith in God, Samah. I do."

Humbled, Samah took the grapes, trying to enthuse herself with a desire to eat. It was useless. Before long, even Anticus gave up the pretense, and he had the servants clear the table.

Hector came to the door. "General Trajan is here, my lord."

Anticus smiled. "Send him in! Send him in!"

The man who entered the room came as a surprise to Samah. Although he had to be close to fifty years of age, his physique was lean and hard, his hair lightly speckled with gray. His vivid blue eyes were clearly visible across the distance of the room

Anticus rose to his feet, shifting his toga as he did so. "Trajan. It's good of you to come."

"You sent for me, my friend," the other man laughingly reminded, taking Anticus by the forearm.

Anticus returned his laugh. "True, but it was good of you to come when I know you are so busy."

"Never too busy for a friend."

"Cassius is home." The words hung like a threat in the air.

"Ah," Trajan breathed. "I didn't know."

"He came unexpectedly. Titus allowed him to return from Palestine when he heard that I was ill."

"I see." He turned the full force of his blue eyes on Samah. "And who might this be?"

Anticus's look was inscrutable. "She is Cassius's slave, Samah. A Samaritan of the Christian faith who was caught inside Titus's siege wall."

Trajan smiled at Samah, reaching out a hand to her. She took it, and he squeezed it briefly. "A sister in the Lord, then. How wonderful that you escaped Jerusalem."

When he looked into Samah's eyes, his own eyes widened, and the color drained from his face. He stood looking at her for so long that Samah grew uncomfortable under his continued regard.

"From Samaria, you say?" he asked absently.

"Yes," Samah agreed, curious at the man's sudden stillness. "My parents live there."

"Have you an aunt?"

Surprised at the question, Samah nodded slowly. "Yes. Her name is Mara. She's married to my Uncle Adonijah."

Trajan's face paled even further. Growing concerned, Anticus stepped forward.

"Are you all right, Trajan?"

The words seemed to snap Trajan out of the trance-like state he had fallen into.

"Yes." He glanced at Anticus. "Yes, I'm fine."

Anticus motioned to the couch, watching his friend closely. "Have a seat. You don't look well."

Though Trajan was still staring at Samah, he quickly turned to his friend and smiled. "I'm fine, I tell you. It's just the heat."

Lifting one brow dubiously, Anticus seated himself opposite his friend. The fall temperatures had dropped considerably the last several days, causing him to question the statement, but he said nothing. He rang the bell beside him, watching Trajan's still pale face. When Hector arrived, Anticus told him, "Bring some wine, Hector."

"Yes, my lord."

Trajan followed his progress as he left and then turned to Anticus.

"Did you say Cassius's slave?"

When Hector returned with a tray, Anticus took a goblet, motioning for Trajan to take one for himself. Both men relaxed back against the cushions.

"I haven't talked to Cassius about the slave issue yet," Anticus told Trajan. "I'm afraid I need to let him adjust to the fact that I'm a Christian first."

Trajan chuckled lightly. "I assume he didn't take it too well."

Anticus smiled wryly. "Better than I hoped."

Samah watched the two men, so different yet so alike. From time to time, Trajan's eyes would stray to her, and she squirmed under his look, not certain what to make of his continued perusal.

She let her mind wander to thoughts of Cassius, and wondered where he was and what he was doing. She prayed for his safety and his acceptance of his father's faith. She only hoped that Anticus's faith in her was as justified. Frankly, she doubted her ability to reach Cassius if his own father could not.

"Where is Cassius now?" Trajan inquired, setting his goblet back on the table.

"Right here."

The cold, clipped voice caused the smile to falter and then die on Trajan's face. He rose to his feet, studying Cassius warily.

"Welcome home, Cassius."

"Thank you."

Anticus noticed Cassius's bristling demeanor. "Dear, dear," he stated wearily. "This is not exactly as I hoped it would be when I got you two together." At both men's questioning looks, Anticus pursed his lips, shrugging. "I have something I need to say to the both of you."

Samah saw Cassius's eyes darken to ebony, and she felt her own stomach drop in expectation of what was to come.

"More bombshells, Father."

Looking uncomfortable, Trajan glanced from one to the other. "Really, Anticus, whatever you have to say should best be said between the two of you."

Anticus shook his head. "No, this involves you, too, my friend."

Trajan sank to the couch behind him.

"Come, Cassius. Have a seat," Anticus demanded.

"I think I would rather stand."

Anticus steadily regarded his son until Cassius finally yielded. "Have it your way then. Let's get this over with. I suppose it has to do with this confounded religion you've all embraced," he snarled, glaring at Trajan.

He seated himself beside Samah, giving her a brief look. Turning back to his father, he impatiently prompted, "Well?"

Without preamble, Anticus told them, "Cassius, Trajan is your true father."

seven

For several long moments both men stared at Anticus, doubting his sanity. The lasting silence in the room became almost oppressive, an eerie tension hanging in the air.

Cassius was the first to break it.

"What are you saying?" he choked out.

Anticus took a deep breath, glancing guardedly from one to the other. He began to nervously twist the purple fringe on the edge of his toga. "It's a long story," he finally told them.

"I have time."

Samah looked quickly at Trajan's set white face. His features seemed carved in lines of marble, his jaw clenched firmly. Though his voice had been quiet, it was menacing nonetheless.

"As do I," Cassius agreed.

For the first time since Anticus had made his declaration, both Cassius and Trajan looked at one another. Both men seemed to be searching for something in the other that would give truth to Anticus's statement.

Cassius turned back to Anticus, fear radiating from his dark gaze. Anticus had always been his father, the one who loved and cared for him. Though he knew that Anticus was not his blood father, it had never made a difference in his feelings for the older man. Would such a revelation fracture the bond that had always existed between them?

As though he could read Cassius's mind, Anticus smiled reassuringly. His own eyes shone with a love that nothing could sever. Somewhat satisfied, Cassius awaited Anticus's explanation.

Anticus focused his unwavering gaze on Trajan, an imploring look in his eyes.

"My friend, I never wished to deceive you."

Brushing both hands slowly through his hair, Trajan held his head between his palms and studied Anticus.

"How can this be true?" he asked through clenched teeth.

Slightly embarrassed, Anticus looked quickly at Samah before flushing a bright red. He returned his gaze to Trajan.

"Perhaps you don't even remember Cassius's mother. She was the wife of General Florian."

Startled, Trajan straightened. "I remember her," he disagreed huskily. "I didn't know she was married at the time. When I found out, I left."

Anticus nodded. "Indeed. You left shortly thereafter for a post in Jerusalem, and Callista found out she was pregnant with your child."

Trajan's lips parted slowly, his tongue brushing his suddenly dry lips. "I never knew."

Again, Anticus nodded. "Callista told me the father of her child and promised me to silence. I know I shouldn't have agreed, but she was desperate."

Cassius felt Trajan's look, and turned slowly to face him.

"I can't believe it. Cassius is my son."

Cassius couldn't believe it either, but after careful contemplation of the other man, he could see similarities that he hadn't really thought about before. The thought of being an illegitimate child, though, left a sour taste in his mouth. But would it be better to be legitimate and rejected? He smiled without mirth.

"I have always thought of you as a man any other man would be proud to claim as father, and I have always been pleased to call you my uncle, but this is something I need to think about."

Rising to his feet, he motioned to Samah. She quickly got up, steadying herself with her crutch.

"Wait!"

Trajan rose to his feet also, standing almost toe-to-toe with Cassius. "We need to talk."

Cassius shook his head, his mouth set grimly. "No, now is not the time. My father," he said with intent, glancing at Anticus wryly, "has given me much to think about today. I need to be alone."

"When can we talk, then?"

Taking Samah by the arm, Cassius began to walk away. Without looking at Trajan he replied, "I'll let you know."

Cassius maintained a brooding silence as they walked along the streets. Darkness had descended, and the carts and wagons were making their way through the city streets to the markets to unload their supplies for the morning. A watchman passed them, his alert soldier eyes searching for anything improper.

Samah longed to offer Cassius some kind of comfort, some kind of counsel, but she could think of nothing to say.

There was something about the man Trajan that bothered her. His eyes continually strayed her way the whole time they were in the room together. It caused the hair to prickle on the back of her neck.

Democritus met them in the atrium. "My lord, Justinian is awaiting you in the peristyle."

Frowning, Cassius snapped, "Now?"

Surprised, Democritus took a hasty step backwards. "I'm sorry, my lord, but he thought you were in a hurry."

Sighing, Cassius looked at Samah. "Come with me."

She followed him in silence. When they entered the garden, Justinian turned from his contemplation of the fountain in its center. He smiled.

"Ah, my lord, you've returned. I hope it was all right with you that I waited here. Democritus seemed to think that you would return soon."

Cassius unhooked his cape from his chest piece and dropped it on a marble bench. "I hope you haven't had to wait too long."

Justinian made a disparaging gesture. "Not at all."

Motioning for Samah to be seated next to his cape, Cassius

turned to Justinian. "What do you have to show me? I must say, it didn't take you long."

Chuckling, Justinian carefully removed a leather thong from a pouch. "It was a challenge. I couldn't sleep for thinking about it."

He took a block of wood shaped somewhat like a foot from the same bag. Kneeling before Samah, he glanced at Cassius first for permission. Cassius nodded for him to continue, watching with interest as Justinian placed Samah's leg into the top portion of the wood piece. A piece of lamb's wool was fit into the hollowed out surface of the wood, and Justinian placed Samah's leg there. Her leg slid smoothly into the groove, fitting snugly. Justinian then took the leather thong and wrapped it around the whole piece, much like any other sandal.

When he finished, he sat back on his haunches and glanced up at Samah.

"Stand up," he commanded.

Easing herself to her feet, Samah stood for the first time evenly with both appendages on the ground. Her eyes widened in surprise, and she smiled brightly at Justinian.

"Try to walk," he told her calmly.

Hesitantly, she moved the encased foot forward, then pulled her good foot forward to meet it. Though it was awkward, she was able to maintain her balance without the crutch.

Cassius stood watching her silently, his arms crossed over his chest. He caught Samah's eye.

"Well," he asked. "What do you think?"

"I. . .I don't know what to say."

"Can you use it?"

She took several more steps, and though the fitted piece was awkward, it gave her more freedom of movement than the crutch. She assumed she would grow accustomed to it in time, just as she had her crutch.

Smiling shyly from Cassius to Justinian, she told them, "It's a marvelous invention."

Justinian beamed at them both. "Does it meet with your approval, my lord?" he inquired at length.

Cassius gave him a brief smile. "I knew if anyone could do it, it would be you, Justinian." The carpenter's chest puffed out proudly at the honest praise. "Come with me, and I will get your payment." He turned to Samah. "Wait here."

Samah seated herself on the marble bench, stroking Sentinel's massive head. What Cassius had done for her was a marvelous thing. She felt a thrill of happiness at being able to walk unencumbered by a crutch. She wondered why he would bother to do such a thing. Alerted to his return by the dog's attentive posture, she smiled shyly when he came through the door.

Though Cassius seemed pleased with his gift, it was obvious that his mind was on other matters. As for herself, Samah was reluctant to mention his comments about repayment. She had no money to give him, and her mind balked at payment of any other kind.

Cassius came and stood before her. Samah had to look a long way up into his face.

"I was hoping the sandal would give you more freedom of movement. Try it for a few days, and if things work well, I would very much like it if you would take Sentinel for walks around the city, much like you did in Caesarea."

She blinked wide eyes at him. "Is this the. . .the payment you spoke of?"

One corner of his mouth tilted slightly, and there was a devilish sparkle in his eyes. "Of course. What did you think I meant?"

Disconcerted, Samah ducked her head in embarrassment. "I had no idea, Tribune."

Cassius smiled at the rosy color flooding her cheeks. Her dark brown hair tumbled around her face, hiding her features from him. Wanting to see her face, he dropped to one knee before her.

"Samah," he entreated softly. "Look at me."

She had a hard time doing as he suggested. Finally, she lifted her eyes to his. He reached out and traced a finger slowly down the creamy skin of her cheek.

"You have nothing to fear from me. I will not hurt you."

Looking into his handsome face, it suddenly occurred to her that he could hurt her in ways he was totally unaware of. She knew with quick insight that she loved him as she had never loved any other. Swallowing hard, she dropped her eyes to the floor.

Cassius studied her a long time before rising slowly to his feet. He hadn't missed the softening of Samah's features, and he felt his heart beating more rapidly in response. He had seen that look before, and knew with certainty that Samah was infatuated with him. For the first time in his memory, he found himself reluctant to hurt a woman.

"Take some time and get used to the shoe. There are things I need to attend to."

"Are you going to speak to your father?"

Seeing his darkening expression, she realized she shouldn't have spoken.

"What I do is of no concern of yours," he told her coldly. "I'm leaving Sentinel with you. See that he is fed."

"Yes, Tribune."

Cassius saw the pain flash through her eyes and knew that he had hurt her. His own distress had caused him to lash out in anger, and though remorseful, he really didn't know what to say. Besides, she was a servant and nothing more. Why should he even care what she thought?

"And by the way," he told her roughly. "The title is now Commander."

"Yes, Commander."

He barely heard her softly spoken answer. Shrugging off the feeling that he should somehow remedy her unhappiness, he turned on his heel and left.

❧

Cassius watched the full moon rise above the eternal city.

Sitting on a hill not far from the Tiber River, he knew the golden globe would be reflected on its glistening surface. He was smart enough to sit upwind, for the Tiber reeked of the city's waste that was piped from Rome's homes.

A cool breeze wafted gently on the night air, lifting Cassius's dark curls from his forehead. He tensed at the sound of someone approaching.

"I thought I might find you here."

Trajan's voice came to him from the darkness, followed by the man himself. Cassius said nothing.

"Do you mind if I have a seat?"

Without looking at the other man, Cassius told him, "As you wish."

Undaunted by the lack of welcome, Trajan seated himself next to Cassius. Taking a blade of grass, he began to chew it.

"I remember how often you used to come here to think."

Cassius remained silent.

Sighing impatiently, Trajan dropped the blade of grass. "Has it ever occurred to you, Cassius, that this might be just as big a shock for me as for you?"

Acknowledging that to be so, Cassius relaxed slightly. He asked the question that plagued him the most.

"Did you love my mother?"

Trajan took so long to answer, Cassius turned to him with lifted brow. The older man shrugged.

"I thought so," he answered quietly.

"You *thought* so?" Though Cassius hadn't raised his voice, Trajan flinched at the angry retort.

"I was very young when I met your mother, and full of life and Roman pride. She was very beautiful." He paused. "But then I found out that she was the wife of General Florian."

"And you were what? A captain?"

He nodded. "Needless to say, when I found out that Callista was the wife of my superior officer, I left."

"Would you have done so if you had known about me?"

"I don't know." Trajan's voice was ragged. "I keep asking

myself the same thing."

"You have never struck me as a coward," Cassius disputed.

"There are differing degrees of cowardice, Cassius," Trajan disagreed. "I'm not certain what I might have done."

Cassius remained silent, his questions unasked. Suddenly, he was afraid to know the answers. Indeed, as Trajan had said, there were different degrees of cowardice. He had never considered himself to be afraid of anything, but now. . .

"Where do we go from here?" he asked the older man.

Trajan turned to him, his look direct and unyielding. "Where do you want to go from here?"

Cassius couldn't hold his gaze. He looked back to the rippling surface of the Tiber reflected by the moon's bright light.

"I don't know. To me, Anticus is my father, and always will be."

"That's understandable. Perhaps we could go on as we have been." His voice grew soft. "I have always loved you, Cassius."

Love. The mere word left Cassius feeling cold. "As you loved my mother?"

Trajan smiled slightly, wrapping both muscular arms around his pulled-up legs. " 'If I speak in the tongues of men and of angels, but have not love, I am only a resounding gong or a clanging cymbal. If I have the gift of prophecy and can fathom all mysteries and all knowledge, and if I have a faith that can move mountains, but have not love, I am nothing. If I give all I possess to the poor and surrender my body to the flames, but have not love, I gain nothing.' "

The words, spoken with such authority, moved Cassius's heart, and goose bumps appeared on his sun-darkened skin. Narrow eyed, he studied Trajan.

"What kind of love are you speaking of?"

Trajan took his time answering. "There is a love that is greater than all loves. When you ask if I loved your mother, you speak of one kind. I could not love your mother as I love you. The two are incomparable."

Anger flashed from Cassius's eyes. "I hear it in your voice. You have answered my question. You *did not* love my mother. She was nothing more than a. . .a diversion."

"That's not true. I honestly thought that I loved her."

"Then how do you know you didn't?"

Trajan plucked a small rock from the ground and sent it sailing towards the river. It rippled the surface with unerring accuracy.

"I met another woman some time later. Her image has stayed in my heart ever since. I have never been able to love another, and what I felt for your mother pales in comparison."

"This woman," Cassius ground out. "Why didn't you marry her? What happened to her?"

It took some time for Trajan to answer, and then his voice was laced with regret. "She was married."

Cassius snorted. "You seem to have a desire for other men's wives."

The dry tone of Cassius's voice sent the color flooding to Trajan's cheeks. Suddenly, he got to his feet.

"Think what you like, Cassius, but it doesn't change the fact that I love you. In my heart, you have always been a son to me."

Instantly repentant, Cassius rose beside him. His own feelings were in utter chaos, but one thing he knew with certainty: He still felt a great love and respect for Trajan. "I'm sorry. I have always felt the same way about you, and though I can't see you as my father, I can still see you as my friend."

Cassius slowly held out his arm to the other man, and Trajan hesitantly clasped his forearm. A silent message of understanding passed between them.

"You spoke of another kind of love? What were you talking about? And what is this about angels, prophecies, and burning flames? When you spoke, you sounded almost like an oracle."

Trajan smiled slightly. "Another time, Cassius. You have too much on your mind now to be able to understand such mysteries." He turned away and started down the hill. "Besides, your father should speak to you first."

Cassius watched him walk away and felt sudden fear grip his heart. His father? What was Trajan talking about? What would Anticus know of the prophecies Trajan was speaking of?

He gave up trying to sort it all out. His mind was numb from thinking. Right now, all he wanted to do was to go home and sleep. Perhaps he would awaken in the morning and find that it was all a dream.

Turning, he followed Trajan's steps back down the hill.

❧

Democritus showed Samah where the scraps of food for Sentinel were kept. Seeing the great quantity of waste, she couldn't help but think what such "rubbish" would have meant to the starving people of Jerusalem. Shaking her head at such morbid thoughts, she fixed a plate and laid it before the dog. Democritus watched her skeptically.

"I'm telling you, he won't eat. He has never eaten for anyone except the master."

Sentinel sniffed the plate and then began eating hungrily. Democritus's eyebrows flew upwards in amazement.

"I can't believe it." He eyed Samah suspiciously. "How did you manage it?"

She didn't know how to answer him. A slight grin tugged at her mouth when she thought of explaining angels to his untutored mind. She shrugged her shoulders.

Still doubtful, Democritus glanced from the dog to the girl. It was obvious that he thought her some kind of sorceress. When he finally left them in the kitchen, Samah sighed with relief.

Pulling a chair next to the table, Samah picked a peach from the wooden bowl resting there. She munched on the fruit while she watched the dog. Glancing down at her foot, she smiled softly.

She thought again of the generosity behind Cassius's gesture. Already she was growing accustomed to the false foot, and it did, indeed, give her more freedom. It was like having a new life. If only her parents could see. A familiar pang of loneliness ran through her.

When Cassius had knelt before her to promise her that he meant her no harm, she had noticed something lurking in his dark eyes that left her vaguely unsettled. Could she trust him to mean what he said? Could she trust herself? There was that in his look that sent her heart thrumming in response. Was it truly fear she felt, or something else?

After Sentinel finished eating, she took his plate and washed it, returning it to its place on the shelf by the door. She stood in the kitchen and turned in a complete circle, making certain that nothing was out of place. Satisfied, she held out her hand to the dog.

"I suppose you are to stay with me," she told him, smiling. "Well, then, let us go to my room so that we may retire for the night."

Since she had no lamp for light, she used the bright light of the moon to prepare herself for the night. She replaced her tunic with a softer, lighter one meant for sleeping. Climbing onto her couch, she pulled a sheet over her and settled down for the night. Sentinel came and lay on the floor at her feet. Sighing, he placed his head on his paws.

Samah turned her look to the moon, visible outside her bedroom window. Its brightness added shadows to the interior of her compartment, giving the room an oddly menacing appearance. Reaching down to where Sentinel lay, she stroked his head, feeling suddenly protected.

Lord, she prayed. *Why am I here? What do you want me to do?*

When she thought of the fate of her people, she could only be thankful that Jehovah had spared her. But why? What did the Almighty want her to do in this heathen city, among this heathen people?

Words her parents frequently spoke came to her mind now. *We must seek and save the lost.*

There were certainly enough of those in this evil city, but

what could one person do? Then, as if the Lord spoke clearly to her mind, she remembered story after story about the apostle Paul. He had reached out to the Gentile people, and they had responded by the thousands. The world was truly hungry for a savior. Hadn't Jesus Himself said so?

The harvest is plentiful, but the workers are few.

She must be an open vessel that the Lord could use for his own purpose. She must be ready to speak when the opportunity arose. And above all, she must stifle this mind-numbing fear that gripped her when she thought about those who had been martyred before her.

Her eyes closed, and sleep came. She was unaware of Cassius coming into her chamber and staring down at her or of his commanding Sentinel to stay. For a long time the commander watched her sleeping. He reached out a hand and lightly traced her soft lips, causing her to stir restlessly.

Pulling his hand away, he turned and left the room.

eight

For the next several weeks, Cassius left Samah entirely alone. Any demands he had on her time he relayed through Democritus. Though the Greek slave was ambiguous in his feelings towards Samah, he was meticulous in her care. Since Cassius thought so highly of the girl, the slave would do his duty by her.

Daily, Samah walked stiffly along the streets of Rome, her unusual gait causing many eyes to turn her way. Still, it was her flawless beauty that made them turn a second time, their eyes following her progress through the busy streets. Only the huge beast ambling at her side kept many from approaching her.

Unmindful of the speculative looks she was receiving, Samah enjoyed the days of leisure with Sentinel as her companion. She was fascinated by the vast array of goods offered in the market, and they often spent their time wandering through the forums.

Sometimes Democritus would give her a coin and ask her to purchase things for him. Samah thought it fun to haggle with the vendors, and she grew adept at outmaneuvering them in their prices. More often than not, one look into her gentle eyes would cause a merchant to suddenly drop his price. Unaware that this was the case, Samah thrilled at her good fortune.

The agony of the separation from her homeland and family began to diminish to a dull ache. Though she continued to pray for her family, her past became almost dreamlike, the present her only true reality.

The fall air had a chill to it today, and Samah was thankful for the warm clothes that Cassius had provided her with. She tugged the warm cloak about her shoulders and pulled the dry flowers in the beds out and threw them into a pile.

She was working on the bougainvillea bushes when Anticus

came to see her. He looked old and worn, lines carved deeply along the sides of his mouth. When he smiled, though, the years seemed to drop away.

"Hello, my dear. How are you today?"

Uncertain of how to respond, Samah hesitated. Though Anticus often treated her like a daughter, she was still nothing more than a slave.

"I am well, my lord."

Anticus glanced around the garden. "And where is your protector today?"

Frowning slightly, she told him, "Sentinel is with Cassius."

Anticus crossed the garden to stand before her. His eyes searched her face thoroughly for a long moment. Seemingly satisfied, his smile grew larger.

"I have come to speak with you about my son."

"My lord?"

Taking her by the hand, he pulled her to the marble bench. Releasing her hand, he seated himself and patted the marble beside him. "Come, Samah. Sit with me awhile. I need someone to talk to, and I think you are just the person."

Puzzled, Samah waited for him to continue. Anticus adjusted his toga comfortably and then turned to her.

"I praise God that He sent you to us. If anyone can reach Cassius with God's word, it will be you."

Surprised, Samah shook her head. Anticus stopped her when she tried to speak. Holding up a hand, he told her, "No. Don't interrupt. Let me finish."

Lifting her hand into his, he smiled slightly. "Even the Lord wasn't accepted by His own family until after He died. Families are strange that way. Fathers and sons especially. I think it has to do with the male ego and not showing weakness before someone you look up to."

Samah returned his smile, squeezing his fingers gently. "I have thought the same myself. Too often someone turns away from the truth because they fear looking weak to those closest to them."

"You are very wise for your years, my dear." He cocked his head to the side. "How old are you?"

Nonplused by this turn of the conversation, Samah stammered, "I. . .I'm twenty years of age."

"Cassius is twenty-two, did you know?"

Searching her mind for a response, she finally settled for a shrug. "No. I did not."

"Only twenty-two years of age, and already a commander in Rome's army. Quite an accomplishment, is it not?"

Thankfully, he didn't expect an answer. Eyes shining with pride, he continued.

"He has shown himself to be fearless among the enemy." The smile suddenly dimmed on his face. He looked past Samah, a faraway look on his face. "But he is still afraid of death. At least where I am concerned."

"He loves you very much," Samah told him softly.

Anticus returned his look to her. Sadness etched his features. "I am still going to die." Seeing her distress at this abrupt statement, he patted her hand. "Now, now, my dear. You of all people should know this is not a bad thing. To be with Christ Jesus is something to look forward to. My sadness comes from knowing that I probably will not have the time to convince my son of God's love."

Samah didn't know what to say. The paleness of Anticus's skin and the lines graven into his face spoke of the progressiveness of his illness. His dark eyes, so full of life, reached out to her with hope.

"But you, Samah, you will have the time I do not."

Getting up from the bench, Samah twisted her fingers in agitation. Her voice was full of anguish. "But what can I do? I am only a slave."

Frowning heavily, Anticus made a tisking sound with his tongue. "And that is something we must remedy, also. To be a slave of Christ is one thing, but a slave of man is something else entirely. I will have to speak with my son about this."

"You will have to speak with me about what, Father?"

Both Samah and Anticus jumped at the quiet voice. Though his face was without expression, Samah wondered just how much of their discussion Cassius had overheard.

Anticus glared at his son. "Really, Cassius. You might give someone a little notice of your arrival."

Lifting one brow arrogantly, Cassius looked from one to the other. "Unless something has happened in my absence that I am as yet unaware of, this is still my villa."

Samah cast her eyes to the ground, her body tensing at the coldness of his voice. "If you will excuse me, my lord."

"No, I will not," he told her inflexibly. His eyes wandered over her in slow perusal, causing butterflies to flitter through her stomach. "I would like to hear more of this conversation that I interrupted."

Samah quickly lifted her gaze, and then dropped it again. Cassius stood like some silent statue, his uniform giving him the appearance of an unyielding warrior. Sentinel stood by his side. The two of them presented an awesome front, and Samah could well understand why Cassius had made the rank of commander so young.

Undaunted by his son's brash behavior, Anticus smiled. "I have not seen you lately, Cassius."

Flushing slightly at his father's intended rebuke, Cassius pulled his gaze away from Samah and concentrated on his father.

"I have been busy."

"Ah, I see."

Anticus looked his son squarely in the eye, his knowing look making Cassius squirm with guilt. Knowing that his father had a penchant for making him feel like some misbehaving schoolboy, Cassius quickly took the offensive.

"Since you are here, why don't you come into the triclinium where it's more comfortable. I will have Democritus bring us some refreshment, and we will continue this. . .um. . . most interesting conversation."

"I would like that," Anticus agreed placidly.

Cassius spoke to Samah without looking at her. "You, too."

Her blood seemed to turn to ice. Regardless of what Anticus believed about his son, and regardless of her own confused feelings where he was concerned, Samah was still wary of the Roman. When he looked as he did now, she could believe him capable of anything.

Anticus settled among the cushions on one of the couches, while Samah stood uncertainly nearby. Seeing her standing there, Anticus motioned to the seat beside him.

"Come, my dear. Have a seat."

She glanced fearfully at Cassius, but his face revealed nothing of his thoughts. He nodded permission, and Samah reluctantly took her seat.

Cassius stood before his father. "What is it you wish to discuss with me?"

At his father's pointed look, Cassius seated himself on the couch opposite them. Anticus leaned forward.

"Cassius, my son, I love you."

The quiet words disarmed Cassius as his father had intended. His shoulders slumped in defeat. How could he stay angry after such a proclamation?

Reaching back with one hand, Cassius began to massage the tense muscles of his neck, rolling his head slowly from side to side. Though he answered his father, he couldn't bring himself to look at him.

"I know that." Recognizing Anticus's tactics for what they were, he smiled wryly. "All right, Father. I am calm now. What did you wish to discuss with me?"

"Cassius, slavery is wrong," Anticus stated without preamble.

Cassius leaned forward, impaling Anticus with his suddenly intense gaze. "When did you decide this?" he asked slowly. "You have owned slaves for years."

"When I became aware of how much God loves His people, I set my slaves free."

Samah could see from the shocked look on his face that Cassius was trying to analyze what Anticus had just told him. Cassius's face darkened.

"This Christian religion you've embraced. That's what this is all about, isn't it?"

Anticus looked at his son sadly. "How can I tell you? It is so much more than a religion. It's a way to spend eternity with the One who created the universe."

Thinking he understood, Cassius breathed out slowly. "Father," he said softly. "I know that you want to believe that there is life after death, but it's just not so."

"But it is! God has given us a way to be with Him for all time. Only man's sin keeps him from being in the presence of God. He loves us, Cassius. He made a way for us to go from being illegitimate children to being coheirs with His only Son."

The reference to illegitimacy stung. "You are speaking of my being a child of an illicit affair."

Realizing his mistake, Anticus paled. "No, my son. I was not referring to just you, but to all of us."

"All of us? All of us *Romans* you mean."

Samah's quiet voice interrupted the tense exchange.

"My lord, every person born is an illegitimate child."

At Cassius's glacial stare she was reluctant to continue, but with a nod, Anticus urged her on.

"The Lord Jesus, God's true Son, told us that every man that is not for Him is against Him. There are only two masters in this world: God and Satan. If you don't serve God, then by your very denial you must serve Satan."

"Satan?" Though confused, Cassius was intrigued by what she had to say. "Who is this Satan?"

Samah sighed. "It's a very long story."

"I like stories." Cassius's voice was glacial. Feeling her stomach begin to churn, Samah had to take her courage firmly in hand. Haltingly, she began to tell the story of creation and the fall of man. She took him through the prophecies in Scripture, all the way to Christ's birth and death, and finally to His resurrection.

Democritus came in to light the lamps, and Cassius noticed for the first time the darkening shadows in the room. It had taken more time than he had imagined for Samah to finish her tale. He glanced at his father.

"And you believe all this?"

Samah's heart sank. Had he heard nothing, then? Would he believe it all just a fanciful story?

There was a resolute look of faith on Anticus's face. "It's hard to explain, Cassius, but when you accept it as fact, and do as the Lord commanded, your heart is suddenly filled with peace. Somehow, you just *know* that it is right."

"And this Jesus was a Jew?" Cassius demanded, his smile dubious. "Yet the Jews have slaves of their own. Is slavery then only forbidden to Gentiles?"

Anticus shook his head. "No, Cassius. Jesus came to fulfill the word, and to change the world. The life He suggests would make the world a perfect place."

"Are you then perfect?" Cassius asked, glancing from his father to Samah skeptically.

Samah answered. "No, my lord. We are made perfect by His blood, but we are still an imperfect people. Jesus told us to be perfect as the heavenly Father is perfect."

Cassius rose to his feet and began to pace the floor. "So He wants you to do the impossible." He stopped and glared at both of them. "And you are willing to follow such idiocy?"

"Cassius," Anticus cajoled. "Have there not been times when your commander has told you to do something that you thought was impossible?" Seeing that Cassius realized the truth of the statement, Anticus continued. "Did it stop you from following orders? Did you tell him you couldn't and that it would be *idiocy* to follow him? Of course you didn't. You continued on. They didn't expect you to win, but they did expect you to *try*."

Cassius looked from one to the other. "Your religion is a religion of paradoxes. It's a wonder that anyone believes such a thing."

Anticus's shoulders sagged in defeat. Looking tired and worn, he got slowly to his feet.

When he saw his father's sadness, Cassius regretted speaking so bluntly. Better to let his father believe in some insane religion that would give him peace and offer him hope. Truth to tell, he longed for such himself.

"We haven't eaten yet," he told Anticus, his eyes filled with worry. "I'm sorry. It's late, but I forgot to call for supper."

"I'm not hungry. Thank you anyway. I think it's time for me to go home now."

Cassius strode to the door. "I'll call for a litter to carry you."

"No."

Anticus's defiant voice stopped Cassius in his tracks. He looked questioningly at his father.

"I will not be carried by slaves." Adjusting his toga over his shoulder, he told Cassius, "I'll walk."

"Over my dead body."

The two glared at each other, both angry and determined to have their own way. Anticus knew he hadn't the strength to push his son, but Cassius knew also that he hadn't the will to truly defy his father should he decide to be stubborn.

Samah tried to soothe the situation. "Perhaps a hired litter."

Cassius glared at her, and she withdrew into silence.

"A splendid idea," Anticus agreed.

Rolling his eyes towards the ceiling, Cassius slapped his palms against his thighs. "By the gods!" His glare turned on his father. "So be it. If it will appease your conscience, then by all means pay my slaves to carry you."

Anticus looked as though he were about to argue, then thought better of the idea. Smiling, he nodded. "Agreed."

Cassius glanced at his father suspiciously, but chose not to argue further.

He helped Anticus into the litter. "I will come by tomorrow to see you. I leave for Palestine again in a fortnight."

Shocked, Samah clutched her tunic to her chest. Palestine. Home! Would he take her with him? Hope spiraled in her heart only to be doused at his next statement.

"I'm leaving Sentinel with Samah. The two of you can enjoy long theological discussions together."

Though Cassius's voice was laced with sarcasm, Anticus smiled at the idea.

"I would like that. How long will you be gone this time?"

"I don't know. A band of Jews have barricaded themselves in Herod's stronghold at Masada. Titus is determined that they shall not defy Rome."

Anticus nodded. "I know the one. An impregnable fortress." His eyes took on a decided twinkle. "Another impossible task, Cassius."

Instead of being offended, Cassius laughed. "We shall see."

Anticus watched his son intently. "Nothing is impossible for those who believe," he said softly.

Tilting his head slightly, Cassius regarded his father soberly. There was more to his words than what was on the surface. "I'll remember that."

After Anticus departed, Cassius returned to the triclinium. Samah started past the door when he halted her.

"Come inside, and we'll have something to eat."

Samah hesitated. "You wish me to bring you something to eat, my lord?"

"No," he disagreed testily. "I wish for some company."

Since he had avoided her for some time, Samah could only suppose that this sudden request had to do with what his father had said earlier.

"As you wish."

Feeling uncomfortable, Samah reclined on one couch while Cassius reclined on the other. His unwavering gaze was unnerving.

Democritus brought them food, his eyebrow lifting when he noticed Samah on the couch. He placed the tray of food on the table before them.

"Is there anything else, my lord?"

"No, Democritus. You may retire for the night."

Democritus glanced from one to the other. "As you wish, my lord."

Cassius noticed the color bloom in Samah's cheeks at his continued regard. Smiling slightly, he tried to put her at ease. He really did want to have her company. She fascinated him, more than any woman ever had. He was intrigued by her acceptance of her fate without any anger or bitterness. The woman positively radiated with joy, and that very light attracted him.

Setting his wine goblet on the table, he asked her, "This God of yours. Why did He let His Son die? And on a Roman cross?"

"I told you. It was necessary for Him to sacrifice His own life so that we all might have life in Him."

Cassius understood sacrifices. Even the Roman gods received their portion of appeasement.

"From the story you told me, one would wonder why your God would put such a tree in the garden to tempt this Adam and Eve. Without the tree, there would have been no need to sacrifice His Son."

Samah picked at the fruit in front of her. Why did Cassius want to ask her such things now? Was he truly interested, or was there some ulterior motive? With Titus's capturing of the Jews, the arena games had begun again in earnest. Was he trying to trap her in some way? Even so, she must use this opportunity wisely.

"God wants us to obey Him freely. All He asks of us is obedience. Had there been no tree, there would have been no choice, and God would have had only a child's doll to play with." She dropped the grapes back to the tray and looked at him. "Like Sentinel."

A leg of chicken halfway to his mouth, Cassius slowly replaced it on the tray. Samah knew by the way his eyes darkened that she had angered him.

"Sentinel was free to go. He chose to stay."

"And you appreciate that faithfulness. You care for him as most people care for their children. Like God cares for His children. But what of Democritus?"

At his sudden stillness, Samah decided she had spoken too freely.

"Continue," he demanded softly. "What exactly do you mean?"

Deciding she had gone too far to retreat, she asked him, "Is Democritus free to choose whether he goes or stays?"

"He's a slave."

Samah nodded. "Had God not given us the choice, that's what we all would be. Nothing more than slaves. He didn't want slaves who served Him out of duty and fear. He wanted children who would serve Him out of love." She paused. "Sentinel serves you because he loves you. But what of Democritus?"

He looked at her strangely. "What of *you*?"

His soft words had a strange effect on her midsection. She sat up abruptly. "What of me?"

He wiped his hands on a towel then dropped it on the table, never taking his eyes from her. Getting up, he crossed to where she sat, and sat down next to her. He was so close, she could smell the sandalwood fragrance that he liked to use in his bath.

His face was only inches from hers. "If I gave you the choice, would you flee back to the hills of Palestine?"

Turning her face away from his concentrated gaze, she looked at her fingers twisting ineffectually at the tie to her tunic. He placed his hands over hers, stilling them with his warm touch.

"Look at me," he commanded.

Samah had to force herself to obey.

"Would you leave me and go back to your home? Do you serve out of duty?"

Samah swallowed hard, forcing down the lump in her throat. She licked her dry lips and noticed his gaze focus there.

"What. . .what do you want me to say?"

Though he was known to be a woman hater among his

men, Cassius had to admit that the thought was very far from his mind right now. What did he want her to say? That she loved him? That she served because she wanted to please him? But would that be true? It came to him with sudden clarity what she was trying to say about her God. Cassius didn't want Samah's obedience because she feared him; he wanted her to truly care.

But if he wanted her to care, what did that say about him? Were his own feelings growing even though he tried to deny them? Or was it something more basic? He was her master, after all, and despite her deformity, she was a beautiful woman.

It had been a long time since he had desired any woman. Now, he found himself thinking about Samah more than he cared to admit. He wanted her, and this frightened him more than anything had in his lifetime. Facing enemies in battle was as nothing in comparison. The thought of having a relationship with a woman, a lasting relationship, left him weak in the knees.

Samah saw the flame of desire leap into his eyes, and she pulled away. For the first time, she became truly afraid of what Cassius might do. She stood suddenly.

Surprised, it took Cassius a moment to realize her intent. He reached swiftly to stop her, but she eluded his grasp.

Samah began to back towards the door. "Do I have a choice?" she asked, her voice hoarse with emotion. "Am I allowed to choose whether I go or stay?"

Cassius rose to his feet. Her words hit him like a dousing of ice water, and his ardor cooled. They stood facing each other, both of them breathing hard.

'No," he told her adamantly. "You have no choice."

"I thought not," she told him, tears in her eyes. "Then give your hollow commands! I'll obey, because I must. But for my Lord, I obey because I love Him."

Turning, she fled from the room.

nine

Cassius stood staring out the bibliotheca window, his mind wandering from subject to subject. The beauty of the garden outside failed to soothe him as it normally did. Whichever way he went in his thoughts, they determinedly returned to Samah.

He didn't want to admit it to himself, but the feelings he had for her were growing deeper. More complex. She was unlike any woman he had ever known. What was there that made her so different from the others?

Perhaps it was her genuineness. Her smiles were real, her feelings honest. There was no hypocrisy in her anywhere. This was something he had never encountered before. Women were known for their guile.

Before he had suspected even Samah, but now he found himself doubting his original judgment. Was it because his feelings towards his own mother had mellowed in the face of the new information he had received about her? Or was it because of Samah's own gentle personality?

He had been wrong. So wrong. Guilt settled heavily around him like a shroud.

Democritus tapped at the door. "Master?"

For the first time he could remember, the word grated on Cassius's nerves. Master. Slave. There was nothing wrong with such an arrangement, was there? Slavery had existed from the beginning of time, even among the Jews.

"What is it, Democritus?" he asked without turning from the window.

"General Trajan is here to see you."

Cassius felt his stomach knot with apprehension. He hadn't been able to face Trajan since that night by the river because he wasn't exactly certain how to act towards him. He just couldn't bring himself to think of Trajan as his real father.

Cassius sighed. "Bring him in."

Trajan hesitated at the doorway, uncertain of his welcome. He stood tall and straight, his toga tucked into the crook of his arm. Cassius smiled and moved forward, hand outstretched.

"Come in and have a seat."

Noticing the scrolls scattered across the desk, Trajan hesitated.

"You're busy. I can come back another time."

Cassius shook his head. "No. I was just reading over some old manuscripts. I think I was seeking some form of diversion."

Trajan studied him. "You need diversion?"

Cassius scraped a hand back through his dark hair and turned away. Lifting one hand, he twisted the bulla around his neck that had been given him when he was a few days old. Though the charm had remained around his neck since that time, it had done nothing for his peace of mind. "I need something. I think I will go insane if I can't shut the thoughts out of my head."

Trajan seated himself beside the desk and picked up a scroll. He looked at Cassius questioningly. "Homer? Not exactly light reading."

When Cassius turned and leaned his back against the window, the sunlight illuminated his features, revealing the haggardness of his expression. He shrugged, avoiding eye contact with the older man.

"Do you want to talk to me about it, Cassius?" he asked softly.

Cassius stared at him, remembering the times that he had confided in him. For years, Trajan had been his confidant, always there when he needed someone to talk to. But now, he didn't know what to think.

Trajan sat quietly, not pushing for confidences. He waited until finally Cassius breathed out heavily and dropped into the chair opposite him.

"I don't know where to begin."

Still, Trajan waited.

Cassius looked to the ceiling, his teeth grinding together. When he glanced back at Trajan, there was a mixture of hurt and anger in his eyes.

"My mother. All this time I have blamed her for abandoning me." He grabbed a scroll from the desk and crumpled it in his hand. Throwing it across the room, he glared at Trajan. "And all this time, Anticus knew. All this time, I've taken my anger. . .my hatred out on other women."

Trajan moved the rest of the scrolls on the desk out of harm's way. His look was full of uncertainty.

"That decision you made on your own."

Annoyed, Cassius glowered at him. "You think that I don't know that?" He pushed himself to his feet and returned to the window. He couldn't look Trajan in the face.

"And then there's you."

"What about me?"

Cassius clenched his fists against the windowsill. "I don't know how to treat you. What to say to you."

Trajan came and placed a large hand on Cassius's shoulder. "Cassius," he scolded lightly. "I am still the same man that you have always known. As I told you before, you have always been a son to me in my heart. Knowing that it is truth only makes me that much prouder. To have sired a son such as you would make any man proud."

Cassius froze beneath his hand. He turned his head slowly and looked into Trajan's eyes, and knew he spoke the truth. The love was there for him to see. The frozen spot in Cassius's soul melted ever so slowly. Turning fully, he forced himself to walk away.

"What is it that's truly bothering you, Cassius?" The pain from Cassius's rejection was evident in Trajan's voice.

"I'm illegitimate. I was never meant to be."

His choked voice brought Trajan once again to his side. "That's not true. God meant for you to be, or you wouldn't exist. Only He has the power to create life." He paused. "As for the other, many children are illegitimate, and they still have good lives."

Angry, Cassius faced him. "God! How does it always come back to God? I assume you mean the Jewish God you and my father have spoken of," he sneered.

"There is no other," Trajan answered quietly.

Cassius returned to his seat, picking up the stylus used for writing. "You know," he said, his voice full of doubt, "I've never really believed in anything but myself."

Trajan smiled wryly. "And how does it feel being your own god? Never needing anyone, or anything. Totally self-sufficient."

Cassius's face flushed with color at the sarcasm. If only that were true. He turned pleading eyes to his birth father, not really knowing what he wanted to say.

Trajan remained standing near the window. "There is a God, Cassius. And He loves you."

Cassius's eyes narrowed with suspicion. "How did you come to believe in this God? I assume it was when you were in Palestine."

Trajan turned his eyes away. "I was in Jerusalem."

Cassius leaned back in the seat. "Ah, yes. After you left my mother."

Frowning, Trajan met Cassius's narrow-eyed gaze with one of his own. "Let's not return to that subject. I will not continue to apologize for something I was unaware of." His voice grew soft. "I have repented of my sins, and God has forgiven me. It does no good to relive your mistakes over again."

"Was it in Jerusalem that you met this other woman you have never been able to forget?"

Trajan paled. "Yes. Well, actually I met her in Samaria."

"And did you know she was married when you fell in love with her?"

Trajan's brows wrinkled. "I can't remember. I knew it shortly thereafter."

"And is she the one who introduced you to this Jewish God?"

Throwing Cassius a knowing look, Trajan smiled slightly.

"Yes, in a manner of speaking. I arrested her husband and brother-in-law. We had a chance to talk."

"Talk?" Cassius lifted a brow dubiously.

Trajan's face flushed with anger. "Yes, talk."

Cassius studied him thoughtfully. "But you wanted more, didn't you? I can see it in your eyes."

Trajan remained silent.

"And she taught you about this God of hers?"

"Let's just say, she pointed the way."

"And what has this God done for you, Uncle Trajan?" Cassius asked softly, mindless of using the loving title.

Crossing the room, Trajan seated himself across from Cassius once again. His eyes were filled with an intense light.

"Oh, Cassius," he breathed in wonder. "If only you knew. My soul is finally at peace. Jesus, the Son of God, died so that we might be reconciled with our heavenly Father in eternity. He is one Father who will never let you down."

Cassius threw the stylus to the table. "He seems to have let Samah down."

Trajan smiled with understanding. "But things are not always what they seem." He dropped his gaze to the table. "She reminds me much of Mara."

"Mara?" Cassius frowned. "That's what Samah said her aunt's name is. She told me she has a birthmark on her face that makes others afraid of her."

Cassius caught Trajan's eye and knew with sudden certainty that the Maras were one and the same.

"I see," Cassius said heavily.

Trajan continued to regard him steadily. "I would like to purchase Samah from you."

Cassius's face darkened with anger. He rose slowly to his feet, his hands clenched at his sides.

"I thought slavery was wrong. What was it you called it? A sin?"

Trajan pursed his lips, picking up the stylus from the desk and turning it methodically in his fingers. When he glanced at

Cassius, Cassius's eyes narrowed.

"I see. You would free her." He angrily jerked the stylus from Trajan's fingers, leaving a slight gash. Seeing the trickle of blood, he burned with shame, but couldn't bring himself to voice his regret. He went to the door and yelled for Democritus.

"Yes, master?"

"Bring a bandage. The general has cut his finger."

Looking past Cassius's shoulder, Democritus saw the slight swelling of blood. Turning, he hastily departed to do as bid.

Cassius returned to the table but didn't seat himself again. His dark countenance spoke clearly of anger held tightly in check.

Trajan broke into his thoughts.

"I would do more than free her," he told Cassius calmly. "I would return her home."

The anger exploded. "I just bet you would. And then you could see her aunt again. Well, let me tell you something. She's still married."

Trajan remained unaffected by his outburst. "I didn't say that I would return her myself. I'm well aware of the temptations involved. Regardless of what you may think, Cassius, I *do* have some scruples."

They stared at one another for a long minute. Cassius finally spoke with deadly quietness.

"I won't let her go. She's mine."

Opening his mouth to speak, Trajan was interrupted by Democritus.

"Here you are, my lord."

Trajan took the cloth from the slave and wound it around his finger. He looked at Cassius, wanting to say more.

"Democritus," Cassius hastily interrupted, "show the general out, please."

Recognizing the undercurrent of tension flowing between the two, Democritus hurried to obey.

Trajan followed him out the door but then turned back.

There was a challenging glint in his eyes.

"I will be praying for you, Cassius. God hasn't finished with you yet."

His prophetic words hung in the air long after he was gone.

❧

Samah knelt beside the small rabbit and loosened the snare from its leg. She could feel its little body shivering beneath her carefully exploring fingers.

The animal was in shock, that was obvious. Its huge black eyes stared vacantly in Samah's general direction.

"It's all right," she soothed quietly. "It will be all right now."

She continued to stroke its downy fur until its heaving sides quieted somewhat and its eyes began to focus once again. She watched its twitching nose, wrinkling her own in return.

Placing it on the ground, she patted its furry backside.

"Go on. Go home."

"What are you doing there?"

The wrathful voice brought Samah whirling to face the intruder.

A large man stood beside a small cart, a whip dangling from his fingers. His eyes sparkled menacingly. Inside the cart lay the corpses of several small animals, and she realized that the snare must belong to him. Swallowing hard, she faced him unflinchingly.

He moved purposefully towards her. When he drew abreast of her, he allowed his gaze to slide over her. The angry sparkle in his eyes was replaced with something much more ominous. It was then that Samah remembered that Sentinel was not with her. Cassius had taken him along when he went to the forum to hear one of the senators speak, and he had cautioned Samah to stay close to the villa. But it had been such a beautiful day, and she had wandered much farther than she had intended. The green hills surrounding Rome had beckoned her onward, and she had left the city far behind.

The man standing before her smiled lecherously, his blackened teeth causing her stomach to lurch. Ragged clothes hung from his portly frame, and his foul breath so close to her face caused her to hastily step backwards.

He reached out a hand to steady her, but she slapped it away.

"Don't touch me."

The smile dropped from his face. He looked her over once again before demanding, "Do you know what I could do to you for stealing from my traps?"

Samah regarded him steadily, though her nerve was fast fleeing.

He reached for her again, pulling her close against him. Grinning at her ineffectual squirming, he told her, "Now be a good little girl, huh?"

Shoving her arms upwards, Samah began to pummel him in the face with her fists. Surprised, he let go of her, and she fell to the ground. She glared up at him angrily.

"Why you little. . .I'll teach you!"

Lifting the whip, he brought it down forcefully across her shoulder. The stinging pain brought a small cry from her, and covering her head, she tried to pull away from the fast raining blows.

When they ceased suddenly, she hesitantly raised her head. A man in a billowing black cape stood not more than twenty feet away watching them.

The trapper stood, mouth agape, watching the figure glide smoothly towards them. When the stranger was not more than ten feet away, he pulled a long curving knife from the sheath at his side.

The stranger's eyes shone with intent through the dark burnous that surrounded his face and head. His look never wavered from the trapper.

"Go," he hissed, and needing no further bidding, the trapper fled into the surrounding forest, leaving his cart behind.

The man in black looked at Samah, and she felt her insides coil at the coldness of his gaze. Returning the knife to its sheath, he moved slowly towards her. He reached down a hand to her, but she drew back as though stung.

"Come," he commanded.

Samah crawled backwards away from him. "No! Stay away from me."

He closed the distance between them. Reaching down again, he lifted her by the shoulders until her face was close to his. Though she couldn't see his face, his eyes were lifeless. Cold. It was like looking into the face of death.

"Please. Let me go."

"I have come for you, Samah, sister of Ramoth."

Shocked, Samah hung limply in his arms. "Ramoth? You know Ramoth?"

He nodded.

"But how? I don't understand. Ramoth is in Samaria."

"I haven't time to explain. You must come with me now. I have been watching you, waiting for the opportunity to reach you."

The words caused Samah's eyes to widen. *Watching me how? Where?* Slow tingles of fear spread across her body.

Confused, she didn't know what to do. *Was this man really sent by my brother? And if so, was Ramoth here in Rome?* The thought brought terror to her heart.

Before she could decide, a snarling growl brought both their heads snapping around. Sentinel stood mere feet away, his lips curled back over his fangs. Cassius stood quietly at his side.

"Let her go."

The command was quiet. Eerily so. The stranger measured his two opponents before slowly releasing Samah from his grip. He pulled a small knife from beneath his cloak, flipping it in the air and catching it by the blade.

Though Cassius was unarmed, he faced the dark stranger fearlessly. His blood raced through him hotly, readying him for battle.

Sentinel took a step forward, his growls intensifying. Never having seen the animal in such a state, Samah became alarmed. The dog was ready to kill.

It seemed an eternity that the three faced each other in an indecisive standoff. Finally, the stranger threw his knife.

Everything happened so fast that Samah was unclear exactly what transpired. She heard her own scream, saw Cassius turn swiftly to the side in time to keep the knife from hitting him in the chest, and saw Sentinel lunge forward.

Though the knife missed Cassius's chest, it pierced his shoulder, sending him spinning to the ground.

"Sentinel!" he barked, and the dog froze, allowing the stranger to disappear into the darkening forest.

Samah rushed to his side. Dropping to the ground beside him, she reached for his shoulder, only to have him push her hand away.

Gritting his teeth, he pulled the knife from him, and Samah used her cloak to wrap the wound. She looked into his eyes, her own filled with fear.

"We have to get you to someone who can look after you."

"What were you doing out here?" he asked angrily, noticing the ragged tears from where the whip had lashed her tunic. "Thank the deities Sentinel was able to pick up your scent. I wondered what had set him off."

"I'm sorry."

"Sorry?" he exclaimed. "You could have been killed!"

"There's no time for that now," she argued hotly. "We have to get you to a physician. We can use the cart."

"And where in Jupiter's kingdom did you get a cart?"

Helping him to his feet, she allowed him to lean on her to get to the cart. Already the loss of blood was leaving him pale and weak.

"It's not *my* cart." He lifted one eyebrow, but chose not to comment. He lay down, his breathing becoming more labored. Frightened, Samah turned the cart, ignoring the lifeless animal bodies within.

"Sentinel, come."

The dog ran to her side, and even hurrying her steps, it took her some time to reach the city gates. A soldier stopped her.

"No carts allowed until sundown," he told her.

Samah pointed to Cassius's now unconscious form. "I know, but this man is hurt."

Glancing at her skeptically, the soldier moved to the rear of the cart. He looked surprised, then he glared at Samah.

"It's Commander Cassius. What happened?"

Wringing her hands, Samah pled, "Please, he needs a physician."

The soldier noticed the blood-soaked wrap on Cassius's shoulder. He started to reach out, but was stopped by Sentinel's blood-curdling growl.

"Sentinel, stay," Samah commanded, and the dog reluctantly obeyed. The soldier yelled to a compatriot, "Justus, come help me. Commander Cassius has been hurt."

Justus hurried forward, his mouth opening in surprise when he saw Cassius. He looked from the soldier, back to Cassius.

"I'll have to get help to carry him. We can't take the cart inside the city."

The soldier agreed. "Hurry." He turned to Samah, his brown eyes full of suspicion. "You can come with me."

Hoping that he would take her to Cassius, Samah quietly obeyed.

ten

Samah sat on the bench outside the physician's house watching as soldiers entered and left. Sentinel sat at her side, his alert head following the movements of those around him. The soldier named Justus stood nearby watching him warily.

After some time, Cassius stumbled out of the house, several soldiers following close behind.

"But Commander, you are not well enough to leave," one man protested.

Cassius's eyes searched until he found Samah and Sentinel. Relaxing slightly, he moved towards them.

"You are all right?" he asked quietly.

Samah got quickly to her feet. She frowned at Cassius's pale face. "I am well, my lord, but you should not be up and about."

He looked at her tattered clothes, and his eyes grew stormy. Moving the material to the side, he could see the sliced skin beneath.

"Who did this to you? The sicarii?"

Sicarii? Samah remembered the name for the political assassins in Palestine. The dagger men normally worked undercover among the crowds, using the great numbers of people as a shield to hide their swift murdering of victims with their concealed knives. They were revolutionaries who slew Jewish high priests and others who supported Roman rule. *But what would a sicarii be doing this far from home?* she wondered. *Do they believe I am somehow connected with those who supported Rome? Were they trying to kill me? And what of my brother Ramoth? What had he to do with such men?*

Unable to make sense of her thoughts, she reluctantly told Cassius of her encounter with the trapper and the subsequent events, leaving out only the stranger's mention of Ramoth.

Turning, he gave a description of the trapper and the stranger to the two soldiers behind him. "Find them and arrest them."

Snapping a salute, they turned as one. "Aye, Commander."

Cassius noticed the world begin to tip crazily around him. Leaning heavily on Samah, he told Justus, "Get me a litter."

Justus hesitated, then swiftly turned to do as bid. Samah helped Cassius to the bench she had vacated earlier. Leaning his head back against the cool stone building, he sighed with relief. He turned to Samah.

"It would seem your God has watched over you again. I am grateful."

Samah froze at his words.

"We should offer a sacrifice," he muttered roughly, closing his eyes.

Taking a deep breath, Samah murmured, "The only sacrifice He will accept is your life."

His eyes flew open at that. "A little drastic, don't you think?" he asked sarcastically.

She turned and looked him full in the face. "He watches over me because I have already given Him my life. He loves me, and wants to care for me."

"It was not your God who took a blade for you today," he argued angrily.

She looked away, watching the soldiers and people who moved about the streets before the physician's door. Darkness was descending, and most were hurrying home to their suppers and bed.

"Why did you come after me?" she asked softly.

"Because you belong to me."

His arrogance hurt. One corner of her mouth tilted into a sad smile. "But before I belong to you, I belong to Jehovah. You want to keep me safe because you own me, but He wants to keep me safe because He loves me." She looked back at him, studying his now familiar features. "You took a knife for me, and that's a serious thing, I'll grant you; but the Son of Jehovah died on a cross for me. His back was torn apart by the scourging He received, His head pierced by a crown of thorns placed there in mockery. Nails were hammered into His hands and feet, and He was left on that cross to die. Alone."

Cassius could see the tears in her eyes and felt himself go cold all over at her hideous description. Though he had seen many people die in such a way, something about the way she described the scene left him feeling ashamed and distressed.

"Could He not have saved Himself if He was the Son of this God of yours?"

"Yes," she replied quietly, looking up at the darkening sky. "But if He had, we would all be lost. From the beginning of time, through eternity."

He eased himself away from the building and leaned forward. Dizziness assailed him momentarily, then quickly subsided. He found himself caught up in the things she was saying. Something about her words filled him with a hopeful yearning.

"I don't understand. What do you mean by *lost*?"

"Jehovah is light," she told him. "In Him there is no darkness. Sin is darkness. He can have no fellowship with the things of darkness." When they met his, her eyes were filled with entreaty. "We are full of darkness, full of sin; therefore, we are separate from Him. Lost."

He reached out, gently stroking a finger down her cheek. "What great sin could you have committed?"

Her eyes darkened perceptibly, and she moved away from his touch.

"There is no such thing as a great sin. Sin is sin. A lie will send you to Gehenna as quickly as murder."

He smiled a lopsided smile. "And have you lied, Samah?"

Flushing, she cast her eyes to the ground. "When I was younger, many times."

"But no more?"

She shook her head. "No, not since having received Jesus

as my Savior." She looked at him thoughtfully. "If there is a truly great sin, it would be to reject what Jehovah has done for you by rejecting His Son."

"I see." Narrowing his eyes, he contemplated her meditatively. "But if everyone is full of sin, and this God of yours can have no fellowship with such, then how has this Jesus saved you?"

Samah looked for any sign of mockery but could find none. He seemed to genuinely want to understand.

"The blood that I told you about is what saves us. When Jehovah looks at us, He sees us not as we are, but perfect through the blood of His Son."

"Ah, so you do think you're perfect."

She shook her head. "No, I don't. But Jehovah does."

Tramping feet interrupted their conversation. Justus returned with a litter carried by eight slaves.

"Both of you can fit," he suggested to Cassius. "I will go along and see that nothing happens to you."

Too weak to argue, Cassius allowed Justus to help him onto the litter. Samah was then lifted in next to him, and he felt his heart hammering against his chest at her proximity. The mere scent of her made his blood rush swiftly through his veins.

Using his iron will to subject his feelings, he lay back against the cushions and tried to ignore her. Her words kept echoing through his mind. *Sin. Darkness. Blood. Light.*

He fell into a light doze, dreaming of a cross and blood flowing from it into a river. The river surrounded him, and he felt himself drowning. Samah stood next to him, and he could hear her words spoken in Aramaic. *You will be clean. You will be legitimate.*

"My lord?"

Cassius raised heavy lids to find himself staring into a pair of worried blue-green eyes. He lifted a shaking hand to his throbbing forehead and rubbed gently. Slowly, the sensation of being drugged ebbed until he could once again think clearly.

"We are home," Samah told him.

Justus ordered two of the litter carriers to help Cassius inside. Samah followed closely, with Sentinel on her heels.

Democritus met them in the hall, eyes widening in amazement.

"My lord, what has happened?"

"Later, Democritus," Cassius growled. "Just get me to my room."

Leading the way, Democritus hurried into the bedroom and lit the braziers and torches. Democritus gave orders to one of the servants to make certain that the fires in the cellar were kept burning so that the warmth from the radiating heat of the floor would take the chill from the room.

Justus stood at the foot of Cassius's sleeping couch and grinned wryly. "The physician was not particularly pleased with you, Commander."

Cassius snorted. "That the man dares to call himself a physician is a wonder."

"Still, he was right. You have lost a lot of blood."

"And he wanted me to lose more! The next time a physician tries to allow insects to gorge themselves on my blood, I will split the man apart with my sword!"

Justus chuckled. "I agree. I think I will take my chances with the gods."

His words struck a sour chord with Cassius. *What have the gods ever done for me?* he wondered. He glanced across the room and saw Samah standing in the doorway, Sentinel sitting at her side. He almost grinned, for they had the same worried expressions on their faces.

Seeing the two in the doorway, he knew what the gods had done for him. They had brought him love. A love such as he had never expected to receive. But which god—or gods—was responsible?

He caught Samah's eye. *Was it her God that brought us together? And what of Sentinel? Sentinel came into my life long before any Jewish God.*

There were things he needed to think about. To do. But it was becoming increasingly hard to remember.

⁂

Samah watched Cassius's eyes close and remain so. She sighed, moving away from the doorway and back to the atrium. She sat on the edge of the rainwater pool and stared at her reflection.

"Please, Lord," she begged. "Let my seed fall on fertile ground. Open his eyes to Your truth. Let him believe."

Justus came into the atrium. He glanced at the door, but crossed the room to stand beside Samah. He noticed her wooden foot, and his eyes clouded with pity.

He was an imposing figure in his Roman uniform, but unlike many she had encountered, his eyes were gentle.

"The Commander will be much better after a few days rest."

"I know."

He cocked his head slightly, wondering at her certainty. Smiling, he bid her farewell and left.

Democritus peeked his head in the doorway. "The master will most certainly sleep until morning. If you wish, you may take the time to do as you please. I will not need you." He frowned. "And if you could get Sentinel to leave the master's room, I would be most grateful."

Samah hid a grin. It was well known that Democritus was terrified of the dog. Having Sentinel watching him move about Cassius's room would more than likely put the Greek on edge.

Samah entered Cassius's room and crossed to the bed. The peaceful look on his face reminded her of a sleeping infant. Smiling, she pushed his dark hair away from his forehead, noting that his forehead was still cool. Thankful that no fever had set in, she praised Jehovah silently.

Turning to Sentinel lying at the foot of Cassius's bed, she commanded him softly, "Come, Sentinel. Your master is safe, and you are only in the way."

At first, she thought he wouldn't obey, but then he rose reluctantly to his feet. He followed her out of the room, stopping on the threshold to look back at Cassius's sleeping form.

Samah knelt beside the huge beast. Rubbing his ears, she told him, "He will be all right. Democritus will look after him."

When Democritus saw them enter the atrium, his face registered his relief.

"I will be going out, Democritus," Samah stated. "I will take Sentinel with me."

"At this late hour?" he asked, his surprise obvious.

"There is something I must do. I will be safe with Sentinel along."

She pulled her cloak from the hook on the wall, wrapping it snugly around her. Democritus was frowning at her.

"I don't think the master would approve."

Samah smiled at his obvious distress. "I will be fine." She hastily exited the villa before he could change his mind about letting her go. Slipping through the dark streets, she made her way to a familiar dwelling. Though most houses around were already dark, this one spilled light from its small windows. She knocked on the door and waited.

The door opened a crack, and then when she was recognized, much wider. Jonah smiled at her.

"Welcome, little sister. We didn't think you were going to make it tonight."

Samah took his outstretched hand. "I didn't think so, either. My master has been injured, and I needed your prayers on his behalf."

Instantly concerned, he pulled her into the room. "Come in. We'll tell the others." He noticed Sentinel sitting in the doorway. Having grown accustomed to the dog's presence, he motioned with his hand.

"You, too, my friend."

Samah entered the small apartment, her eyes widening at the roomful of people. There were more men, women, and children than before, and she realized that Jehovah was making use of this small body of believers to reap in the harvest of those looking for a savior. Almost all were Gentiles.

Some were ragged, others wore the purple-trimmed robes of the aristocracy, but one thing they all had in common: They welcomed her with smiling faces. She felt the tension slide from her body. Being with other believers had been what had helped her to keep her sanity through the past months.

"Samah has something she wants to say," Jonah told them.

Samah told them what had happened to her on the hill just outside the city limits, only with them, she included mention of her brother.

An older man nodded wisely. "It sounds like sicarii, all right. But what would they want with you?"

"Maybe they believe that since you survived Jerusalem and left with one of Rome's most noted soldiers, you are a sympathizer, or maybe even a spy."

Jonah nodded. "Tamar may be right, but what has that to do with her brother, Ramoth?"

"Maybe they've killed him, also."

The words turned Samah's blood to ice. She shook her head slowly. "That can't be. I don't believe that is so."

Recognizing her anxiety, Jonah held up a hand. "Whatever it is, Samah needs our prayers. Come, let us join together and petition Jehovah on her behalf."

He led the group in a prayer, their voices lifted high in supplication. When they were finished, Samah felt truly at peace. Surely Jehovah would keep watch on her as He always had. The more things that happened to her, the more she believed that to be so.

A young man named Lysus led them in a favorite song of praise. Though Samah felt like shouting the words, she kept her voice low, as did the others. There were still many in Rome who would like to see the Christian community decimated, so the believers continued to worship in secret.

When it came time to leave, Jonah's sister Capua stopped Samah at the door. She waited for the others to go before telling Samah, "Jonah and I would like it very much if you could come for supper two nights hence."

Seeing the affection reflected in Jonah's eyes, Samah hesitated. She had no desire to hurt Jonah, nor Capua, but if the young man saw in her something he wished to possess for his own, she must not allow him to believe it could be so. Her heart was firmly fixed on another, though she often wished it otherwise.

"I don't think so," she answered Capua softly and regretted the hurt that flashed through Jonah's eyes. He had been kind to her, and she hated to disappoint him. "Since my master is ill, I don't know if I will be free."

"You could let us know," Capua argued.

Samah knew she should just say no and be done with it, but she hadn't the heart to do it. She nodded. "All right. I'll let you know."

"You can tell me when you come to the market tomorrow," Jonah told her, his eyes shining.

Since it was her regular day to visit the market, she agreed. Looking past them to where Sentinel sat quietly watching her, she commanded, "Come, Sentinel."

The dog lumbered past her, and she followed him outside. She turned when she reached the street and found Jonah still watching her. Blushing, she gave a brief wave and hurried home.

≈

Democritus found Cassius on his feet early the next morning, long before the sun had risen.

"You should still be abed," the servant scolded, retrieving a tunic from the chest against the wall.

Cassius poured water from a container into a bowl. Cupping his hands, he splashed the cold water onto his face. With his face buried beneath his rubbing hands, he grinned. Democritus sounded like an old mother hen at times.

"I have something important to do today. It can't wait."

Dipping his finger into the tooth powder, Cassius rubbed

his teeth clean. He swished some water around in his mouth, then spit into the bowl.

Democritus took the bowl, making a tisking sound. Cassius could see the arguments forming in his eyes but knew he was too well trained to voice them.

He watched the slave empty the bowl into the garden below. Setting the bowl back in its place, he then turned to Cassius.

"If you're going out, you'll need your toga."

Since he was not in uniform, he nodded. "Where's Samah?"

"In the peristyle. Do you wish me to summon her?"

"No, I'll find her there."

When he entered the garden, he found Samah on her knees clearing debris from the flowerbeds. She turned her head, then got quickly to her feet.

"Should you be up, my lord?"

"I'm fine." Though he felt weak, he wasn't about to admit it. If the servants in this house had their way, he would be a spoiled baby.

Realizing the depth of their concern, guilt flooded through him. He had considered them as nothing more than slaves for a long time, though he was genuinely fond of them. It had never occurred to him that they might actually have some kind of affection for him.

Cassius watched Samah move across the garden to the fountain. She pulled several dry bougainvillea leaves from the water and added them to the other debris she had collected.

"I have to go out," he pronounced, and she jerked around to face him.

"But you are not well!"

"I am well enough," he said firmly. "There is something I need to do, and I must see that it's done today. I will have to leave in a few days for Palestine."

Samah could feel him watching her. Did he think that she had anything to do with the sicarii in the woods? Thoughts of the man and his message still left her frightened.

"From now on," Cassius stated firmly, pointing to his dog lying quietly nearby, "I want you to keep Sentinel with you at all times."

The dog lifted his head at mention of his name. As though he understood, his eyes fixed steadily on Samah.

"Yes, my lord."

Laying his toga across an iron railing, he crossed to stand close beside her. When she lifted her eyes to his, Samah was surprised by the emotion lurking there.

"I don't wish you to call me my lord again," he stated quietly.

Her mouth parted in surprise. 'But. . .what shall I call you then?"

"Call me Cassius," he answered softly, rubbing the back of his hand gently down her cheek.

Her stomach lurched within her. "I cannot."

Instead of being angry as she had suspected, he smiled.

"Then how about beloved?"

Eyes wide, she stepped hastily out of his way. He followed. Her heart beat erratically when he looked into her eyes. Taking her by the shoulders, he pulled her to him. He studied her face carefully, as though to commit it to memory, and she returned his scrutiny fully.

Though her mind told her to move away from his descending lips, her body wouldn't heed its message. When his lips finally touched hers, she melted against him. Sliding his hands up her neck, he cupped her face in his warm palms.

When he finally released her, Samah collapsed onto the bench behind her. He stood looking into her eyes, his own carefully guarded.

"We must have a talk," he muttered raggedly. "When I return from Palestine."

Turning, he left her sitting there. Sentinel whined, and she turned her unfocused gaze on him. She stared at him a long moment and then suddenly burst into tears.

eleven

Cassius entered the villa clutching a bulging bag. Democritus met him in the hallway, taking his purple-trimmed toga from his arm. The Greek's eyes studied his master worriedly.

"You are well, master?"

Cassius raised his thumb and forefinger, pinching the bridge of his nose. He was so tired, and his body still felt weak from loss of blood. He lifted his head.

"I am well enough, Democritus. Gather the slaves in the triclinium."

Sudden fear flashed through Democritus's eyes, but he hastened to obey.

Dragging his tired limbs, Cassius entered the room and made his way to one of the reclining couches. He dropped heavily to the seat.

One by one the servants entered the room, each registering different degrees of dread. They remained silent until all had assembled.

"Where's Samah?" Cassius demanded.

"It's market day, my lord. Samah is fetching the items Cleopas needed for our meals."

Cassius straightened, his eyes focused intently on his servant. "She has Sentinel with her?"

He nodded. "Yes, my lord."

Relaxing slightly, Cassius turned to the others. Taking the sack from beside him. He pulled out several rolled-up scrolls. He regarded each servant in turn.

"I have here your letters of manumission. As of today, you are all free men."

Shocked silence met this announcement.

"Should you wish to remain in my employ, I will be glad

to have you, and I will see that you are paid well for your services."

Uncertain faces turned to one another. Finally, Cassius held out a scroll.

"For you, Democritus. You have attended me well, and I feel as though you are my friend. I regret forcing you to serve as a slave."

Democritus slowly reached out a hand and took the scroll. His shining eyes met those of his former master.

"My lord, I have been happy to serve you. I hope that I might continue to do so."

Cassius considered him carefully, then nodded. "I would like that very much."

When he handed out the scrolls, most happily chose to stay in their present positions. A few, though, hoped to return to their countries to try and find their families. Cassius understood.

Their excited chatter as they exited the room brought a small smile to Cassius's face. When the room was finally empty, Cassius had one scroll remaining. He pulled it from the sack unhurriedly. The smile slowly slid from his face. Tapping the parchment against his lips, he stared out the open doorway into the peristyle. Anyone who knew him would never have recognized the stark fear radiating from his eyes.

❧

Samah added the peaches to her basket, smiling wanly at Jonah. He noticed her pale face.

"You are not well, Samah?" he asked softly.

She turned away, unable to look into his eyes. "It is nothing, Jonah. I didn't sleep well last night."

That was certainly true enough, but definitely not the cause of her distress. Cassius's kiss in the garden had awakened her to feelings she wasn't aware she even had. She wasn't quite certain what to do about the circumstances surrounding her life. Suddenly, things had become decidedly complicated.

"You are worried about the sicarii?"

"That, among other things," she told him honestly.

There was a commotion in the street, and they turned to watch a group of men arguing hotly. As more people gathered to watch, the crowd thickened around them until Samah was pressed from all sides.

She could hear Sentinel lashing out at those around him, and though people hurriedly moved out of the dog's way, the crush continued until even the dog was threatened.

"Samah!"

Jonah's anxious face slowly receded as Samah felt herself pushed ever farther away from the dog and Jonah's booth. She found herself on the fringes of the crowd, and she pushed people aside while she tried to backtrack to reach Sentinel. In the next instant, a bag was thrown over her head. In all the hubbub, her scream went unheard.

She was tossed across someone's shoulder, and she could hear the sound of the crowd diminishing. She squirmed ineffectually against her captor, the bag smothering her yells for help.

When they finally stopped moving, she was dropped unceremoniously onto a hard couch. She landed with a thud, the breath temporarily knocked from her body. The bag was lifted from her, and though the room was somewhat dark, she blinked at the sudden shifting from total darkness to semilight.

The burnous-clad sicarii stared down at her, and tingles of apprehension shivered across her body. The deadness of his eyes terrified her.

"What do you want with me?" she asked tremulously, her bottom lip quivering with dread.

"Be silent. I won't hurt you if you remain silent and be still. But if you don't. . ."

He left the threat hanging in the air. Samah swallowed hard, and shrank back against the couch. Though she wanted to ask more questions, she didn't dare. It was obvious the assassin was waiting for someone.

She took the time to study her surroundings. They were in a

small abandoned apartment, its dilapidated appearance adding to her apprehension. Although she knew that others probably lived in apartments close by, the sight of the assassin's gleaming knife kept her from crying out for help.

Hour by hour went slowly by until Samah was about ready to scream with nerves. She wondered what Cassius would think. Would he believe she had run away? Remembering his kiss, her heart sank. Would he think that her reason for fleeing?

The room grew darker as night descended. Still the sicarii refused to light a lamp. His steady gaze never left her, and Samah found herself frozen with fear.

There was a thump at the door, and sliding his knife from its scabbard, the sicarii went to answer it. He waited until there was a second knock of three raps before he slid the bar back and opened the door.

A tall man entered the room, the darkness hiding his features. He wore a short tunic, his face clean-shaven, and his curly, dark hair short against his scalp.

"Is she here?"

Though the words were hissed, there was something familiar about the voice.

The assassin nodded towards the couch. Turning, the man walked quickly towards her, and Samah shrunk back further into the cushions.

"Samah?"

Recognizing the voice, Samah threw herself off the couch and into the man's arms.

"Ramoth! Ramoth, is it truly you?"

He clutched her so tightly, she thought her ribs would break. "Samah! Oh, Samah! Praise Jehovah!"

He buried his face in her hair, and they both wept unashamedly. The sicarii shifted uncomfortably, obviously unused to such emotion.

"You have my money?" he demanded.

Without looking at the man or letting Samah go, Ramoth pulled a bag of coins from his belt. He threw it across the room.

"Here is your payment. Remember, no one is to know."

Without answering, the sicarii left the room. He melted into the shadows and was gone.

Closing the door behind him, Ramoth carefully lit a lamp. He closed the shutters on the window and turned back to his sister.

"You look well." There was a question in the statement.

Samah could say the same. Her brother had always been tall and well built, but always before his strong chin had been hidden by his beard. Now she could only marvel at how handsome he was. She didn't know what to say or where to begin.

"I *am* well." Her voice was still husky with surprise.

He came and stood before her, his dark eyes studying her thoroughly. There was a reticence to him that had never been there before. He had always been her hero, the one who cared for and protected her. Now, he held back.

"You are a slave of a Roman. How can you be well?"

Recognizing the unspoken words, Samah's eyes darkened with anger. "He treats me well."

"How well?"

She stood, glaring into his belligerent brown eyes. "Why don't you just ask what you want to ask?"

His look fastened on her slave bracelet, his nostrils flaring wide. "All right, I will. Are you the Roman's concubine?"

Ramoth saw the hurt flash through Samah's eyes, and his anger deflated. Hers, however, rose to gigantic proportions. As children, he had always been the hotheaded one, and she the calm, controlled one. But when she grew angry, even Ramoth backed off. Now, he recognized the signs by the flashing of her blue-green eyes, and he knew he had made a grave mistake.

Her hand clenched at her side, and Ramoth knew with certainty that she wanted to lay it across his face. He took her by the shoulders to try and calm her.

"I'm sorry," he grumbled, "but the thought of him touching you. . ."

Recognizing the emotion for what it was, Samah released her breath. Ramoth loved her. Had always loved her. His protection had at times been almost cloying, but she had been grateful for it, nevertheless. When she answered, her voice had softened.

"He has never touched me in such a way."

Frowning, Ramoth's narrow-eyed gaze lingered on his sister's face. The softness in her eyes told him something he had hoped was not so, but her words said something else. Seating himself on the couch, he pulled her down beside him.

"Tell me everything."

Samah started at the beginning, and proceeded to do as he asked. Periodically he would interrupt her with questions, but she finally came to events of today and ended her story.

"And what of you, Ramoth? How did you come to be associated with a sicarii?"

He shrugged, refusing to meet her look. "I hired him. The sicarii have eyes everywhere. I knew if anyone could find you, it would be one of them."

"But what of mother and father?"

He flinched. "They don't know."

"But Titus released you. Cassius said so."

"Cassius? You call your master by his name?"

The warning in her eyes forced him to change what he wanted to say. He looked away.

"I knew if father realized that I was coming after you, he would insist on coming, too. I couldn't have that, so I never went home."

Samah sucked in a shocked breath. "You mean they don't know that we're alive? Ramoth, how could you?"

He got up from the couch and crossed to the other side of the room. Turning his head, he glared at her. "They'll know soon enough."

"What do you mean?"

"I mean," he declared quietly, "that soon we will both be back home."

Samah's mouth dropped open. "But how? I'm a slave now, I can't just leave."

He turned, leaning his back against the wall. "You can if I take you."

Shaking her head, Samah frowned in puzzlement. "I don't understand. How did you even know where to find me? How did you get here? And your beard. . ."

He laughed without mirth. "Don't remind me. Anyway, after I was released from jail, the Romans set me free. They thought I was some kind of political prisoner and loyal to Rome. They had me swear allegiance, and then they turned me loose."

Samah rose quickly to her feet, her eyes widened with horror. "You swore allegiance to Rome?"

Frowning, Ramoth moved his hand in a deprecating gesture. "I didn't mean it."

Crossing the room, she placed her hands on his forearms. "But Ramoth, you know that if you swear an oath, you must do all in your power to fulfill it," she reminded urgently.

Angrily, he shoved her hands away.

"I owe Rome *nothing*!"

Samah's heart sank. For years her parents had agonized over Ramoth's impetuous personality and his refusal to submit to authority. No matter how many times they reminded him of the apostle Paul's admonition to submit to the authorities, Ramoth refused to yield. Reminding him that it was a sin did no good, either. It had only caused him to move further away from the Lord.

"Well, I do," she countered softly. "I am a slave, and the apostle Paul said to be subject to my master in everything. If I obey and try to please him, it will make the teaching about God more attractive. Paul said so."

"Paul was never a slave!" he refuted hotly.

Her eyes filled with love. "He was a slave to Christ. Wherever Jehovah sent him, he went, knowing that the Lord had His purpose." She touched Ramoth's shoulder and felt his strong muscles tense beneath her fingers. "Ramoth, Jehovah allowed me to be here for a purpose. I believe that with all my heart, and until Cassius says otherwise, I can't leave."

Grabbing her by the shoulders, he shook her slightly, his voice lashing in its intensity. "You're going, Samah. One way or another."

"She's not going anywhere."

So heated had been their exchange that neither had heard the door open. Spinning around, they stood staring in stunned amazement at the figure outlined in the doorway. Cassius stood there, Sentinel by his side. Four other soldiers stood waiting behind him, their swords drawn and ready.

❧

Cassius watched as the soldiers removed the young man from the room. The boiling rage within him had sought an outlet and had found one when the young Jew had attacked him. With one blow, Cassius had laid him out.

"Cassius, please."

The tears raining from Samah's eyes did nothing towards softening his wrath. "Silence!" he barked, and waited until the room was empty. Taking Samah by the arm, he propelled her none too gently out the door and into the darkened streets.

"Where are they taking him?"

Though Cassius's stormy eyes fastened on her briefly, he never checked his stride. Samah was tempted to do as bid and be silent, but she could not. Ramoth was her brother. She reached out a detaining hand, clutching Cassius's arm.

He whirled on her in fury. When he had at first been apprized of Samah's abduction, he had been filled with a great fear. That fear had rapidly turned to anger when the fruit vendor had mentioned the sicarii. The description was no coincidence. He knew the man must be one and the same as the one who had accosted her on the hill.

"Who is this man? What is he to you? To hire an assassin, he must care for you very much."

"He's my brother," she snapped.

That brought him up short. He sought the truth in her face,

and found it. Some of the anger ebbed. The last he had heard, her brother was still in Palestine. He must have followed them here and waited for a time when he could free his sister.

He glanced behind them, pondering what to do. If anything happened to her brother, Samah would be devastated. Pressing his lips together, he took Samah by the arm once again and propelled her back the way they had just traversed.

They made their way through the streets in silence until he at last came to the garrison where the troops were billeted. Pushing Samah onto a bench, he commanded, "Wait here." He pointed to Samah, and in a barely controlled voice he commanded Sentinel, "Guard."

Samah watched his retreating back, and tried to swallow past the large lump in her throat. Whatever would happen to her impulsive brother now? And Cassius. Never had she seen him looking so ruthless. When he had struck her brother, the resounding blow had echoed in the room. Now she truly feared for her brother's life. Exactly how much of their conversation had Cassius heard?

When Cassius returned, he was followed by two soldiers holding Ramoth up between them. They helped Ramoth to the bench beside Samah. Moaning, Ramoth dropped his head to Samah's shoulder.

"Are you sure about this, Commander?" one soldier asked hesitantly. At a quick jerk of Cassius's head, the soldier sighed. "As you wish. I will have a cart brought around."

Samah stared up at Cassius, her love shining from her eyes. "Thank you."

He glanced at her and turned away. "Don't thank me yet."

She remained silent, wanting to explain, but afraid to do so. When the soldier brought the cart, Cassius helped Ramoth into it, lifting Samah in beside him.

His hands at her waist, he found himself unable to look away from her glowing eyes. Ramoth moaned, and Cassius pulled back. Taking the horse by the bridle, he led them away from the compound.

By the time they reached the villa, Ramoth had come to himself. He clutched his aching head in his hands. Blood still trickled from an open wound on his forehead. Noticing the Roman standing near, he tensed.

"Ramoth."

He jerked his head around at his sister's soft voice, moaning when the bile rose to his throat. She came quickly to his aid.

Placing an arm around his waist, Samah helped him from the cart. "You are at Cassius's home."

Democritus hurried down the stairs, his hands on his hips. "Another one?"

Cassius glanced at him briefly. "Take him inside, Democritus. Find him a room."

When Samah would have followed, he took her by the arm. "Not you. You have some explaining to do."

He pulled her into the triclinium, and shoved her onto a couch. "Well?" he demanded.

She related the story as Ramoth had explained it to her. Frightened of what his reaction might be, she bit her bottom lip and waited for his response.

Sighing, he sat down beside her. "I can't fault him for his desire to rescue you."

"What are you going to do?"

He eyed her casually. "I don't know. But until I decide, I think it might be wise to put your brother under guard. There's no telling what he might do."

Samah couldn't argue with him there. She was just thankful that Ramoth hadn't been sent to a Roman prison.

Calling Sentinel, Cassius left the room, returning moments later without the dog.

He didn't come back to his seat by her side. Instead, he went and looked out the open doorway into the garden beyond. His back was rigid.

"Would you have gone?"

She didn't pretend to misunderstand. She stood and limped across to him. Though she didn't touch him, her words held him tightly in place.

"I told him I could not go unless you gave me permission."

He lifted his head slightly but still kept his back to her.

"And if I gave you that permission? Would you go then?"

Would she? Though she longed to see her home and her family, her heart was tied up with this surly soldier of Rome. How had that come to be? A cruel twist of Jehovah's whim, perhaps. Immediately repentant of such thoughts, she begged forgiveness. If Jehovah wanted her to love this man of Rome, then she had no choice. But did Jehovah truly want her to remain in this country so far from her people?

Cassius turned. "You don't answer. Perhaps that tells me what I need to know."

For the first time, she recognized that she had the power to hurt him. She could see it in his eyes. He truly cared about her, but how much? Would he feel abandoned again if she left him? Would it tear his heart apart as it would hers?

Before she could answer, he moved away from her and lifted a scroll from the table. His eyes meshed with hers, and he swallowed hard. Coming back to her, he held out the paper.

"Perhaps this will help you decide."

She took the paper and looked at it, puzzled. "What is this?"

"Your liberty. It's a document giving you your freedom."

She glanced at him in surprise. Reaching out, he swiftly removed her slave bracelet and the coin from her neck. His face was taut with apprehension.

"I gave all of my slaves their freedom this morning." He brought his face close to hers. Taking her by the chin, he told her softly, "You've convinced me that it was wrong."

She didn't know what to say. "Oh, Cassius."

His name on her lips sounded like music. Cupping her face between his palms, he asked her, "Will you stay?"

A knock on the door interrupted them. Democritus peeked his head inside.

"My lord, Hector is here. Your father is very ill, and he wants to see you."

twelve

The flickering torches on the wall lighted the bedroom. Anticus lay on his bed, his white face pinched with pain. His breathing was labored and shallow, but his mouth tilted into a smile when he saw his son.

Cassius sat carefully on the bed, lifting his father's cold hand into his larger, warmer one. He pushed the silk sheets out of his way, adjusting them over his father for more comfort. His other hand joined with the two, and he began to rub Anticus's hand gently, as though by doing so he could impart some of his own strong life force.

"Cassius, my son."

The voice, though weak, was full of patriarchal pride. Cassius felt his heart give a mighty lurch.

"Father."

Cassius couldn't speak further, a solid lump forming in his throat. His eyes surveyed his father tenderly, and he knew with dreadful certainty that these were his father's last minutes. Tears hung suspended on Cassius's lids.

"Cassius, I must tell you something."

"Shhh, Father. Save your strength."

A smile peeked past the pain in the old man's eyes. "For what? My time has come, and I will soon be with my Lord. It's you I'm concerned about."

There was peace in the look of confidence he gave Cassius, and Cassius marveled at his father's assurance in a Jewish god. He turned his head slightly when he heard a disturbance at the door. Trajan came quickly into the room, assessing the situation in one quick look. His mouth turned down into a frown.

Anticus saw him standing behind Cassius, and he smiled. "Trajan! I was afraid you wouldn't make it in time."

Trajan exchanged a quick look with Cassius and then returned Anticus's smile half-heartedly. "Don't be foolish. Would I let you down?" He held up a hand. "No, don't answer that!" He grinned. "What are you up to, old friend? Have you more information to shock Cassius and I?" he asked jokingly.

Anticus grew serious. "As a matter of fact, I have," he rasped. The smile slid from Trajan's face.

Turning to his son, Anticus looked steadily into his eyes. "Cassius, I have found your mother."

A blanket of silence hung over the room, both men too shocked to respond.

"Hector will take you to her."

Cassius glanced at Trajan, his mouth parted slightly in surprise. Trajan's face had lost its color. He looked back at Cassius, his eyes full of questions.

Turning back to his father, Cassius shook his head. "I don't understand."

"Cassius," Anticus pleaded. "Go to her. Make your peace with her. Allow her to finally give you all the love she has always wanted to." He squeezed Cassius's hand. "Let her take my place in your life."

Nostrils flaring, Cassius drew heavily on his self-control to keep from lashing out. He knew his father was only trying to make things easier. Anticus wanted to see all the loose ends of his life tied securely before he departed to the afterlife. Forcing down the rushing anger, he told his father hoarsely, "No one can take your place."

"Cassius, let her try."

Cassius pulled his hands away, scraping one hand back through his hair. "It's not that easy. You don't know what you're asking."

Anticus looked at Trajan sadly. "And you, my friend. You, too, must make your peace with Callista."

Trajan turned his eyes away.

"I'm dying," Anticus told them harshly. " I want you to promise me now."

Feeling the guilt that Cassius knew his father expected, Cassius pressed his lips tightly together. He wouldn't be coerced into facing his mother. What did he owe her, after all?

Seeing his father's distress at his hesitation, Cassius slumped against the weight of guilt and grief. He might not owe his earthly mother anything, but he certainly owed this man something. More than he could ever repay. If it would make him happy, then so be it.

"I promise."

Trajan came and stood on the other side of the bed. "As do I, Anticus."

Relieved, the old man closed his eyes, sighing heavily. He knew that he had done what he could. Now, only God could make things right.

Leaning forward, Cassius pulled his father's hand up to his forehead. "I love you, Father," he said huskily. "I love you so much."

Pain tore at Cassius heart unlike anything he had ever experienced. Oft times he had overcome physical pain from his many times of battle, but this pain. . .this pain was unendurable.

Anticus pulled his hand from Cassius's and placed it on his downbent head. "And I love you."

The tears that had threatened now found release. Sobbing, Cassius buried his face against the sheets. Anticus continued to stroke his head.

"Remember, Cassius," he said softly. "You have another Father."

Lifting his head, Cassius swimming eyes met Trajan's.

Trajan shook his head regretfully. "No, Cassius. He's not referring to me."

Cassius turned his look on Anticus. The old man smiled.

"Let Trajan and Samah teach you about Him. Listen to their words and heed them." Tears filled his eyes. "Oh, my son! Someday, I hope to be reunited with you in heaven."

Knowing he couldn't promise such a thing, he told his father, "I'll try."

Anticus's body jerked, a spasm of pain crossing his face.

"Father!" Turning, Cassius noticed for the first time the physician standing in the room. "Do something!"

The physician shrugged, hands held out to his side helplessly. "My lord, there is nothing that can be done."

Cassius clutched his father's hand tighter. "Don't die! Jupiter, Juno, and Minerva, save him!"

A slight gurgle came from Anticus's throat. His eyes rolled back into his head, and with a sudden convulsive movement, his body went still.

Cassius felt his father's hand slacken against his. Dropping his head to the sheets, he was helpless against the pain that tore through his own body. His voice lifted in a keening wail. "Noooo!"

❧

Samah entered the room where her brother was being held. She glanced around, noting that the only guard he had was Sentinel, but then she knew that was safeguard enough. The dog watched Ramoth with unblinking eyes.

He was lying on the bed, his arms folded across his chest. Both dog and man looked her way at the same time.

"How is your head?"

Ramoth's eyes were so dark, they were black. "Your Roman has a hefty blow. If I see him again, he will not find me such an easy target."

Samah crossed the room and pulled back the drapes, allowing the cool night breeze to enter the room. "Don't be foolish," she told him in aggravation. "Cassius saved your life."

He got quickly to his feet and started towards her. Sentinel came to his feet at the same time. The dog's fierce growl stopped Ramoth in his tracks. Teeth bared, the animal eyed Ramoth with unconcealed hostility.

Ramoth returned the dog's look warily. "Call him off."

Samah glanced at Sentinel and knew that the animal would never heed her now. "I can't. When Cassius places him on guard, only Cassius can release him."

Frustrated, Ramoth seated himself once again on the bed, and the dog slowly lay back down. He gave his sister a look of extreme ire. He nodded at her foot, his expression sullen.

"What is that?"

Flushing, Samah came and sat next to him. Though Sentinel's ears pricked alertly, he remained still. She reached out to touch the darkening bruise on Ramoth's forehead, but he pulled away. She was unaccountably hurt by his rejection.

"Cassius had a carpenter fashion a false foot." Lifting her leg, she moved the appendage from side to side. "It works marvelously, though sometimes when I use it too much I get a sore on my leg."

Ramoth grunted. He wondered why the Roman would do such a thing for his sister. He studied her now, taking note of the soft clothing and bright colors. It had been almost three years since he had last seen his sister properly. The darkness of the jail cells was barely relieved by the torches on the walls. Then when Jerusalem had been seized, after time, his sister came to him looking thinner, the dark circles under her eyes telling of her malnourishment.

Now color bloomed healthily in her cheeks, her body curved softly with the lines of womanhood. Though she was still a cripple, her beauty was unsurpassed. Many men would overlook such an affliction for such a rare beauty. He thought he knew what the Roman wanted, and the idea made him angry.

"You love him, don't you?"

Casting her gaze to the floor, she twisted her fingers in her lap. It was some time before she could bring herself to answer. He took her by the chin, lifting her eyes to his. He knew she would never be able to lie to him.

"Yes, I do," she told him softly.

Anger caused the blood to flow through Ramoth in a swift flood tide. Reminding himself that it was his own impetuosity that had gotten his sister into this position in the first place, he tried to control himself.

"How could you fall in love with a *Roman?*" he ground out. "Didn't you see what they did to our people?"

She turned her eyes towards him. "How could father love a *Samaritan?* How could mother love a *Jew?*"

Looking ashamed, he turned away. "That's different."

"Is it? Is it really, Ramoth? How so?"

Since Jews and Samaritans had been killing each other for some time, he knew he couldn't win this argument. The story of his parents' own love affair in the face of such adversity still filled him with amazement.

"For mercy's sake, you're a slave!" he finally answered bitterly.

She gave a brittle laugh. "Not anymore."

He glanced at her sharply. "What do you mean?"

She pulled the manumission scroll from her belt and handed it to him. "He gave me my freedom."

Ramoth read the scroll, his eyes widening. He handed it back to her. Perhaps he had been wrong about the Roman after all. "So you're free. Leave."

Samah made a sound with her lips. Her angry gaze clashed with his. "If I didn't leave you alone in Jerusalem, I won't leave you alone here."

He reached for her, saw the dog, and thought better of it. "I can take care of myself! I want you to go home."

"He wants me to stay."

The quiet words hung in the air between them. Several seconds of silence passed before Ramoth could speak.

"All the more reason to go."

She turned to him, her eyes full of sorrow. "He's so close to believing, Ramoth. Someone needs to teach him the way."

"Well, let someone else," he argued angrily. "If Jehovah wants him to be saved, he *will* be."

Not able to look him in the face, she got up and moved away, her back to him. Ramoth wanted to follow, to shake some sense into her, but he knew he wouldn't make it past three steps before the monster watching him would be upon him.

"Did you ever think that perhaps that's why I am here in the first place?" Samah asked him.

"Your emotions are clouding your judgment," he rebutted. "If you are honest with yourself, you will know why you want to stay."

Though she wanted to deny it, Samah knew that she couldn't. Her feelings for Cassius were past denying, but at the same time, they were decidedly ambiguous.

"Sometimes I'm afraid of him," she said without thinking.

Ramoth grabbed the disclosure like a drowning man grabbing a lifeline. " 'Perfect love drives out fear,' " he quoted. "If you *truly* loved him, you wouldn't fear him. I think you're just infatuated."

She turned to him, smiling sadly. "It doesn't alter the amount of pain."

Realizing that she was wavering, Ramoth gave his final argument. "You're so fond of quoting the apostle Paul and his admonitions about obeying the authorities. Then let me quote the apostle Paul to you. He said, 'Do not be yoked together with unbelievers.' That's a command, my sister, not a suggestion."

Samah felt a lancing pain through her heart. What he said was so. She was so fond of pointing out her brother's weaknesses and faults, but what about hers? All of a sudden, she felt a greater affinity for her brother's impetuosity. How had she grown so far from her beliefs in the past months? Somehow, her attention had shifted from her Lord to an unbelieving Roman. Even when she had tried to reason with Cassius, it was because she longed for him to believe. Why? For his true salvation, or so that he would share *her* faith?

She looked out the window and lifted her eyes to the lightening sky. "Oh, Jehovah," she cried silently. "Forgive me. Forgive me."

Ramoth's voice reached her across the room. "The Roman wants you, Samah. I can see it in his eyes."

She turned and leaned her back against the window frame. Her anguished eyes meshed with his. "What can I do?"

He stood slowly to his feet, keeping a cautious eye on Sentinel. "Go home."

"And what about you?"

He shrugged his shoulders. "What can he do to me? I've done nothing wrong, really."

She took a ragged breath. "You think abducting someone is not wrong?"

"*I* did not abduct you. I merely rescued you from someone who had," he reasoned.

"That's a lie."

He sighed impatiently. "Not exactly, and besides, how could he prove otherwise? If you are gone, then why should they wish to keep me?" Casting her an irritated look, he told her, "Think of Mother and Father. Haven't they suffered enough? They need to know that we're alive."

Samah knew his words made sense, but there was something about his reasoning that made her reluctant. They stared at one another for several long moments.

"Go home, little sister," he pleaded softly.

Still reluctant, she held her hands out at her sides. "How? I have no money, and I wouldn't have any idea how to go about arranging for transportation if I had."

"Go to Jonah."

She lifted surprised eyes to his face. Frowning, she eyed him suspiciously. "How do you know Jonah?"

"I don't. I've only heard of him." He sat down on the bed again, eyeing her carefully. "But I understand that you know him quite well."

Her heart jumped and began pounding heavily. "Who told you that?"

"Never mind. Just go to him, and he will help you."

She looked at Sentinel, considering whether the dog might allow her to take her brother with her. If she held the animal, would he turn on her and tear her to pieces?

Ramoth followed her look. Turning back to her, he laughed harshly. "Don't even think about it. Just go. I will follow soon."

Uncertain of his meaning, she obediently moved to the door. She stopped on the threshold, her eyes meeting her brother's.

He smiled grimly. "Just go."

Turning, she left.

ভ

It was late in the afternoon when Cassius returned to his villa. The final preparations had been made to bury his father in a vault outside the city since no one was allowed to be buried inside. He was weary beyond endurance.

Democritus met him in the hall, taking his toga from him. "My lord?"

One look into Cassius's pain-filled eyes, and the servant knew. His face clouded with sorrow.

"I'm sorry."

Cassius gave him a brief nod. Glancing towards the hallway he asked, "How is the prisoner?"

"He has been no trouble. I gave him food."

"Good." Cassius entered the triclinium and dropped heavily onto one of the couches. Rubbing his face tiredly, he told Democritus to send Samah to him. Cassius knew that she had grown fond of his father, and she would be hurt by his death, but he also knew that she would want to know.

"She's not here, my lord."

He raised a brow. "Where is she?"

Looking uncomfortable, Democritus told him weakly, "I don't know, my lord. She came and told me goodbye this morning."

Cassius froze. He lifted his eyes in question. "What do you mean, 'goodbye'?" He could see that the Greek was nervous. Getting quickly to his feet, he strode from the room and into the one where Ramoth was being held.

"Where is she?" he demanded.

Ramoth lay on the bed, his arms folded behind his head. He turned his head slightly and stared at Cassius in amusement.

"Who?"

Cassius crossed the room and in one swift movement lifted Ramoth by the front of his tunic. "Don't play games with me. Where is your sister?"

Ramoth glanced at Sentinel and then back to Cassius. His eyebrow lifted mockingly. Cassius saw the threat in Ramoth's eyes, and without taking his eyes from Ramoth commanded, "Sentinel, go."

Reluctant, but obedient, the dog slowly left the room, turning to look back once before disappearing from view. Cassius leisurely released his grip on Ramoth's garment.

"If you want to fight me," he grated, "then do so."

Although Ramoth was several years his senior, Cassius had no doubt of the outcome of such a fight. Though the Jew was lean and hard, he hadn't the expertise of Roman training.

Ramoth sat back down on the bed, smiling falsely. "I don't wish to fight you, Roman," he lied. "What would that achieve?"

"If I have to find her myself, I will do so," Cassius warned. "Sentinel has done it twice before, and he can do so again."

Ramoth realized the truth of his words. "I thought you gave her her freedom," he questioned, eyes narrowing with mistrust.

Cassius stood glowering at him. It was true, he had given her her freedom, so why did he suddenly feel the desire to revoke that? He could tell that Samah's brother didn't trust him. In actuality, he wasn't certain that he trusted himself. He had just lost his father, he couldn't lose Samah, too.

"Where is she?" he demanded again.

Ramoth stared at Cassius, then slowly lowered himself to a reclining position. He crossed his hands behind his head and looked fixedly at the ceiling without answering.

"So be it," Cassius growled. Turning, he left the room, calling Sentinel to him. He went to Samah's room and found it empty of most of her personal belongings. He was angered that she had left most of the garments he had purchased for her, and grabbing one from the bed, he held it out to Sentinel.

"Find her," he commanded harshly.

The dog quickly left the room and Cassius followed. Opening the front door, he trailed the animal through the city until he came to the open-air market.

Without hesitation, Sentinel made his way to the fruit vendor's booth.

At first, Cassius believed the dog had made a mistake. It was the fruit vendor that had apprized him of Samah's abduction just yesterday. Had it only been one day since Sentinel had followed her trail through the city until he had found her in that slum apartment? It seemed more like eons.

Now, he could see the vendor's eyes widen, not in surprise, but in fear. Frowning, he closed the distance between them.

Leaning on the counter, he asked him, "Your name. I've forgotten it."

"Jonah," he replied, swallowing hard.

Cassius's eyes glittered dangerously. "Well, Jonah, I need some information."

The man paled. "Information?"

Cassius nodded, leaning negligently on the counter. Jonah was not fooled by his quiet demeanor or his relaxed position. Cassius looked like a lion ready to pounce.

"I am looking for the woman you helped me to find yesterday."

"Woman, my lord?"

Cassius's angry gaze impaled him like a javelin. "Don't play dumb with me," he countered quietly. "I know she was here. If need be, my dog can continue the search." He pointed to the fish emblem on the post without taking his eyes from the vendor. "However, there's no telling what else he may find."

Jonah's face turned absolutely white. He vacillated back and forth in making his decision. Controlling his anger, Cassius tried to allay his fears.

"I mean her no harm. She has decided to leave, and I merely wanted to tell her good-bye."

Jonah eyed him sardonically, obviously not believing him.

"Fine," Cassius growled, and turning to the dog, he snapped his fingers.

Jonah knew that if the animal followed Samah's trail, he would lead the commander to a large number of the body of believers. He couldn't allow that to happen.

"Wait!"

Cassius turned back to him.

"She's at my house," Jonah told him reluctantly.

"Take me there."

The command brooked no disobedience. Motioning to a young boy across the street, Jonah waited until he crossed to them.

"Lucius, mind the stall until I return."

The boy glanced suspiciously at Cassius and then nodded.

Cassius and Sentinel followed the vendor until he came to an apartment complex. A bakery was on one side, a tavern on the other.

Entering a stairwell in the middle, Jonah led them up a dark passage until he came to a small door at the top of the stairway. He opened the door and leaned inside.

"Capua, I'm home."

Capua hurried from the back of the apartment, stopping abruptly when she saw Cassius and Sentinel. Her face paled, and she clutched her shawl to her chest. Samah entered the room behind her. Her eyes widened.

"Cassius!"

His eyes focused on Samah, Cassius asked the other two, "Would you please leave us alone for a few moments?"

Jonah's eyes sought Samah's. She nodded imperceptibly. They both left the room, Capua turning and giving one last glance at Cassius. The admiration in her eyes was unmistakable.

Sentinel seated himself in the doorway, and Cassius went to Samah, taking her by the shoulders. There was hurt in his voice when he finally managed to speak.

"You didn't say good-bye."

Samah cast her gaze nervously around the room. She

couldn't bring herself to look at him.

"I didn't know what to say. I. . .I knew you had a lot on your mind." She pulled out of his grasp. "Your father, how is he?"

"He's dead."

The stark words caused her knees to buckle beneath her. Reaching behind her, she lowered herself onto a seat.

When she lifted her eyes to his, Cassius was surprised to find the pain in their depths mixed with joy. He frowned.

"You are glad?"

She shook her head, a sad smile tilting her lips to one side. "For you? No. For Anticus? Yes."

Cassius thought he understood. He seated himself next to her. "You mean because he is free of pain? Yes, I am thankful for that, also."

She looked at him sharply. "He is free from pain, yes, but he is also alive with Christ."

Instead of being angry, Cassius sighed. "I wish I could believe that."

Samah felt hope flood through her. "You can, Cassius. You have faith in yourself, you can have faith in Jehovah, too."

He smiled wearily. "It's not that easy."

Without thinking, she took his hand. "But it is. Faith is a decision, just as love is. You decide in your heart to believe."

His smile was cynical. "Just like that?"

The pain registered on his face, even while something else flashed through his dark eyes. He closed his hand around hers, his look pulling her ever closer.

"Just like that," she answered huskily. "When your general tells you to go fight, and he tells you that he will send reinforcements, you go, believing it will be so. That's faith."

He loosened her hand, placing his palm against her cheek. His searching eyes reached into her very soul, and Samah covered his hand with her own.

"And if you find out that what you believe in is not real?"

"It is," she assured him. "But even if it's not so, what have you lost?"

What would he? He had seen his father die peacefully, his heart filled with hope. What was so wrong with that? Every one needed to believe in something. What had Roman gods ever done for him?

Cassius lifted his other hand and pressed it against her other cheek. He pulled her face close, his eyes seeking something he wasn't certain she could give.

"Don't leave me," he entreated softly. "I can't lose you, too."

Samah looked into his eyes and completely lost her heart. Ramoth was right. Perfect love did cast out fear. From the moment he had walked in the door, she had realized that she was no longer afraid of him. Her whole being had been flooded with joy at his very presence.

Now, she dreaded the feelings he evoked in her. If she stayed, she might very well betray her Lord and everything He had done for her. Her own eyes were pleading when she answered him.

"I can't stay."

His eyes roved her face disbelievingly. Slowly, he released her. Confused by her response, he wanted to take her in his arms and show her that what she said was a lie.

"Why can't you?"

"Oh, Cassius," she muttered raggedly. What could she say? Not being a believer, he would never understand her reasoning. "I just can't. You wouldn't understand."

"Try me."

She pulled back from his anger. It was so very hard to pull her eyes away from his. The misery she saw reflected there shook her resolve. Getting up, she put some distance between them.

"You're not a believer, Cassius. The apostle Paul has commanded that believers not yoke themselves together with unbelievers." She glanced at him, her eyes darkened with her own pain.

He got up and walked to the other side of the room. Rubbing his forehead, he tried to think clearly. An impossible task. When he turned to her, all the past hurts of his life seemed to be manifested in her. Like his mother, she would leave him. The pain of a rejected childhood rose to taunt him again. He dropped his gaze.

"So be it," he told her coldly. Snapping to Sentinel, he walked quickly from the room.

Samah hurried after him, calling to him from the top of the stairs. Looking up, he lifted an eyebrow in question.

"What of Ramoth?"

Jaw clenched, he continued down the steps. His very rigidness told Samah that he would never return, and she felt her heart fracture into tiny little pieces.

"He is free to go," he told her brusquely.

When Cassius arrived back at his villa, he quickly made his way to Ramoth's room. He found it empty.

thirteen

Cassius sat in his father's peristyle, his blank eyes looking out over the immaculately kept garden. His mind wandered over the many years he had spent here as a child and later as a man.

Sighing, he took a deep breath of the cool winter air. He could almost hear the sounds of childish laughter mingled with the louder, throatier laugh of Anticus. He could picture Samah and Anticus huddled together, their faces lit with something he didn't understand. Overwhelmed with grief, he didn't know what to do.

To lose his father and Samah in the same day was more than he could bear. His love for the woman had blossomed unaware, and now he felt even emptier than before. For the first time, he understood what he had done to the women in his life.

But there was a difference. Samah was not untouched as he had been. He had seen the agony in her lovely eyes when she denied him. Perhaps he should have pushed his suit further, but he hadn't been thinking clearly at the time. All he knew was that the pain caused by his father's death had escalated with the loss of Samah.

"Cassius."

Trajan stood in the doorway, his eyes alive with worry.

Cassius glanced at him, then away. "What do you want?"

Though there was no welcome in Cassius's voice, Trajan entered the garden anyway. He came and stood beside Cassius.

"Are you all right?"

Cassius snorted. "All right? What do you think?" He turned, and studied the older man. Though Trajan's blue eyes were filled with grief, there was a peace and serenity that Cassius was far from feeling. It angered him that the general seemed so unmoved.

"I think," Trajan confided quietly, "that if you could only believe in what your father believed in, you would find the tranquility you are seeking."

Cassius got up quickly, moving away. Another minute and he was likely to strangle the older man with his bare hands.

"This religion you have embraced makes no sense. Why should I believe in such nonsense?"

Trajan smiled sadly. "I agree it makes no sense, but it fills your very heart with the presence of God. What sense is there in loving your enemies? In treating kindly those who heap abuse on you? In turning the other cheek when someone strikes you?" He shook his head. "No, it makes no sense. That is, until you understand the great love of a Father God."

Slumping wearily, Cassius turned and searched Trajan's face. "I understand the love of a father," he choked.

Sitting down on the bench, Trajan asked him, "Do you? Do you really? Anticus gave you love, and gifts, and helped you win favor in the Senate and with the emperor. Does that mean he loved you?"

Cassius frowned. "Yes," he replied in confusion. "That's part of it. What exactly are you trying to say?"

Trajan leaned forward, his eyes beseeching. "Who gives you life? Who gives you the very air that you breathe? Who gives you the warmth of the sun, the light of the moon, the beauty of the flowers on the hillside? God does. Does that mean He loves you? Most assuredly, because even beyond that, He gave you the greatest gift of all: He gave you His Son."

Trajan got up and crossed to Cassius's side. Cassius looked at him warily.

"It was so easy for Anticus to believe because he *was* a father. The thought of giving one's own son to die so that someone else might live, he understood that kind of sacrifice. That kind of love."

Casting him an impatient look, Cassius asked, "What

makes you think that this Jewish god is the right one?"

Trajan lifted a brow. "You've been to many lands and seen many gods. Tell me, what kind of life do the people live? What kind of things do their gods teach them? How to kill, like the barbarians in Germania? How to live lives full of lust and debauchery so that they become diseased and wither and die?"

Cassius met his look. "Like Rome, you mean?"

"Yes, like Rome."

Leaning against a railing trailing dry grapevines, Cassius studied his blood father. Memories of long walks among the hillsides and long talks on the banks of the Tiber assailed him. This man had been a true friend to him over the years. A mentor.

"The things you say tear at the very fabric of Rome. Be careful, Trajan, or you might be charged with treason."

Feeling defeated, Trajan sighed. "Then so be it. I promised Anticus that I would try to teach you the way to salvation. You are lost, Cassius, in more ways than one."

Cassius surprised Trajan with his soft answer.

"I know."

"Cassius, if you study Jewish history, you will see the hand of God throughout it."

"Like now?" he asked sarcastically. "It's a wonder that anyone believes in this Jewish God the way He has destroyed His followers."

"The Jews have rejected God's Son, so now He has given up on them and turned to the Gentiles. The Gentiles are hungry for the love of such a God. They see only lives filled with depravity and greed, and they want something more for themselves and their children. God gives them the hope they are seeking, the knowledge that this life is temporary and that there is something much better waiting for them beyond the grave."

Cassius could picture the many people dying in the arena. Many died singing praises to this God, and he had marveled at such a faith. He knew that most Romans would quickly relinquish their worship of any god if they thought their lives were at stake.

Christians would willingly give their lives in defense of their God. His thoughts turned to Samah, and he again felt the pain of her rejection. He could see in her eyes that it grieved her to turn him away, but he knew she would never relent. As surely as a Christian would walk into an arena, Samah would walk away from his love.

Trajan interrupted his thoughts. "Cassius, will you keep your promise to Anticus and go to see your mother?"

Cassius gave him a look filled with aggravation. He really didn't want to think about this now.

"I don't know."

"I'll go with you, if it will make it any easier."

Cassius smiled snidely. "What, a family reunion?" Though he had promised Anticus, Cassius had his reservations about keeping the promise. His guilty conscience smote him, and he realized that he might as well get it over with sooner than later. He crossed to where a large bronze gong sat upright in the garden. Lifting the hammer, he struck it soundly. Hector came at his summons.

"Hector, bring us some wine." Cassius grinned at Trajan. "If I'm going to see my mother, I will need some fortification."

❧

Ramoth stared at his sister and sighed. Over the last week, she had become a pale replica of herself.

When he had made his way to Jonah's house, Samah had been unsurprised by his presence. She told him what had transpired between her and the Roman, and Ramoth had been impressed by his sister's devotion to Jehovah. He supposed he shouldn't have been because it was like having history repeat itself. His own father and mother had walked away from a difficult relationship and for the same reason.

Now he realized the pain it had caused his beloved sister. Her words of commitment to the Lord were more than just words. She truly lived by her faith. Locked in a jail cell for almost three years, he had all but forgotten the truth he had learned from childhood. Samah had brought it back to him with ringing clarity.

She stood on the balcony of the apartment, her eyes gazing towards the part of the city where Cassius lived. Though Ramoth had tried to get them passage on a ship, he had been unable to do so. Most captains were reluctant to sail in the wintertime.

Capua came into the room, her eyes quickly finding Ramoth. She smiled with warmth, flipping her long dark hair over her shoulder.

"Have you ever played knucklebones, Ramoth?"

He shook his head, noticing the bones clutched in her hand. Returning her smile, he told her, "No, I haven't."

"Would you like to learn?"

One of the things he admired about Capua was her lack of artifice. Her brown eyes sparkled with joy and innocence. She and Samah were much alike, and that's probably why they got along so well. Still, he and Samah couldn't impose on their hospitality too much longer.

Calling to his sister, he smiled when she turned to him.

"Capua wants to teach us to play knucklebones."

She returned his smile half-heartedly. "You go ahead. I think I will go for a walk."

Instantly alert, he spoke more sharply than he intended. "Not alone."

Samah regarded him with ill-concealed impatience. "Yes, alone. I won't go far."

He was about to argue with her when Capua laid a hand against his forearm. "Let her go, Ramoth. She will be safe enough on the streets of Rome."

Remembering how easy it had been to abduct her even in a crowd, he doubted Capua's assurances.

"I don't know. . ."

Samah came to him, and laying her hands lightly on his shoulders, she reached up and kissed his cheek. She stared hard into his eyes until he had to look away.

"I'm not a baby anymore," she reminded him.

He grinned. "You will always be my baby sister." Studying her pale face, he finally relented. "Go, then. But if you aren't back within the hour, I will come looking for you."

She wrinkled her nose at him but said nothing. Going past him, she went to her room to fetch a shawl. Ramoth followed her. Expecting more admonitions, Samah was surprised when Ramoth handed her a coin.

"In case you get hungry."

Taking the coin, she then laid her palm gently against his cheek. She smiled into his eyes. "I love you."

He watched her leave the room, his own eyes misty with his feelings.

Samah descended the dark stairway and came out into the bustling marketplace. Uncertain where to go, she wandered slowly along the busy streets.

She passed the fuller's and stopped to watch a servant treading in a mixture that cleaned clothing. Beyond him, other servants were laying togas over frames suspended over fires. The smell of the sulfur used to whiten the garments caused Samah to wrinkle her nose with distaste. She quickly moved on.

She passed two men painting an advertisement for the next week's chariot races on one of the buildings. They paused in their work to watch her walk by, and she felt suddenly frightened. Always before, she had had Sentinel with her. Now, she was alone and vulnerable.

"Samah."

Surprised, she turned to find Trajan not ten feet away. She smiled a welcome. He closed the distance between them, his eyes assessing her.

"Are you alone?"

She shrugged. "As you can see."

He lifted a brow, shifting his toga over his shoulder. "Would you like some company?"

Thinking that he might have some word about Cassius, she hastily agreed. He fell into step beside her.

"How have you been? I thought you would be on your way home to Palestine by now."

"Ramoth has tried, but shipping has slowed to the region since winter has set in."

"I see." He looked down at her. "Did you know that Cassius has been to see his mother?"

She lifted eyes filled with joy to his face. "That's wonderful."

Trajan nodded, his gaze once more forward. He pulled Samah out of the way of a loaded two-wheeled cart being pulled by a young man in an obvious hurry.

"They have finally made their peace with each other. I won't be surprised if Cassius allows her to move in with him."

Shocked, she turned to him. "Things have gone that well between them?"

He nodded again, smiling at her. "Callista is of the Way."

Mouth parted in surprise, Samah felt her heart swell with jubilation. Surely Jehovah was indeed placing people in Cassius's path to bring him to a knowledge of salvation. She prayed for Cassius every day, and it would seem her prayers were coming to fruition.

"And Cassius?" she asked hesitantly.

Trajan grinned wryly. "He is pig-headed, but I see a softening in him."

"Praise Jehovah!"

Trajan looked at her intently. He took her by the arm and pulled her towards a tavern.

"Come and have a meal with me. I'm famished."

Agreeing readily, she waited until they were seated before asking what was uppermost on her mind.

"Cassius, does he still grieve for Anticus?"

Trajan saw the sorrow reflected in her eyes, and took her by the hand. "You truly love my son, don't you?"

Flushing, Samah quickly pulled her hand away. The cacophony of sounds from inside the tavern, mixed with the sounds from outside, made it hard to hear. She caught Trajan's look and realized she didn't need to say anything.

"And he loves you."

Her heart jumped, thrumming heavily in response to his words. She cast her gaze to the table, her finger tracing a carving from a previous customer.

"He has never said so."

Trajan cocked his head slightly. "Did you give him the chance?"

Biting her lip, she leaned back in her chair. She waited until the proprietor had filled their goblets with wine before she answered him.

"He asked me to stay with him. I told him I couldn't."

"Ah." Trajan relaxed back in his seat, eyeing Samah seriously. "And I take it he said nothing about marriage."

She shook her head, not able to look at him.

"Perhaps you misunderstood each other. Maybe you should give him another chance."

She glared at him. "You of all people should understand. Cassius is not a believer."

"Not yet," he said smoothly.

She studied him. "Do you really think there's a chance?"

"I know there is. He was asking me about baptism only this morning."

Samah felt suddenly lightheaded. It would be an answer to her prayers if Cassius could indeed believe, but she suddenly wondered if that would truly have any effect on their relationship. She remembered the hurtful resignation in his eyes when she had denied him. Could he ever really forgive her for that?

They finished their meal and Trajan got to his feet. "Come, let me walk you home. I have a meeting with the solicitor this afternoon, or I would spend more time with you."

She took his hand and allowed him to help her stand. They walked in silence back to Jonah's flat.

Trajan took her hand at the door, lifting it to his lips and kissing it. "Have patience, Samah."

She knew what he meant. She watched him walk away, her heart suddenly light for the first time in days.

৯

Cassius strode along the streets of Rome feeling as though he were walking on air. Trajan had baptized him this morning, and he felt a great sense of coming home. Sentinel walked at his side, his alert ears twitching at the sounds around him.

They had been right, all of them—Anticus, Trajan, Samah, his mother. Accepting on faith that there was one true God and that He had sent His Son to die for the remission of all mankind was easier than he had expected. For the first time in his life, the empty spot within him was filled—filled with a wonderful presence.

Releasing all the pain from past hurts, he had reached out and grasped the hope offered to him. Now, he felt free for the first time in years. Free to love his mother. Free to accept Trajan. Free to marry Samah! It had been three long weeks since he had seen her, and thinking of her now brought that familiar rush of feeling.

He headed for the palace of the Palatine. Emperor Vespasian had requested his presence, and he was in a hurry to see him. He hoped the emperor would allow him to relinquish his command.

He wanted to find Samah and return with her to Samaria. He knew she grieved for her parents, and he was determined that she return as his wife so that there could be no argument against them.

Having been expected, he was quickly ushered into the emperor's presence. Vespasian reclined on a couch, the gold laurel leaf crown on his head reflecting prisms of sunlight when he turned.

He lifted the jewel-studded goblet he was drinking from. "Commander Cassius. Come forth. Join me in a drink."

Cassius hit his breastplate in salute, taking the goblet a servant offered him.

"Your majesty," he said, bowing low.

"Have a seat, Cassius. No need to stand on formality." He motioned to the couch next to him. "My son, Titus, has informed me of your valiant exploits in Palestine. That is why I have summoned you. I want you to return and help Flavius Silva overcome a band of rebel Jews that have barricaded themselves inside the fortress at Masada."

Cassius's heart sank. "But, Your Majesty, I was hoping to be relieved of my command."

Vespasian lifted a supercilious brow. "At the mere age of twenty-two? You have not yet served your twenty years."

"True," Cassius agreed. "But with my father's death, I now have two properties to oversee. There are things that I need to do, and I can't if I am away all the time."

The emperor placed his goblet on the marble table at his side. He turned slowly.

"I heard about Anticus. I'm sorry. He was a good man."

Cassius felt the lump of grief rise into his throat. The wounds inflicted by his father's death were still too raw.

Vespasian considered Cassius quietly for several moments. Finally, he smiled.

"You have done much for Rome, you and Anticus. I will grant you your release from duty."

Relieved, Cassius got to his feet. "Thank you, Majesty."

"Cassius." Vespasian reclined nonchalantly against the cushions of his couch. His dark eyes met Cassius's, and Cassius felt himself go cold all over at the look. "There is something else you can do for me. I have heard rumors of a sect that I thought Nero had destroyed rising again in Rome. They are called Christians. Keep your eyes and ears open, and if you hear of anything substantial, please report it to me."

Cassius wasn't certain exactly what he said, but he found himself dismissed. Hurrying from the palace, he tried to decide his next move.

He must warn the Christian believers somehow. But how? He had no idea where they met.

He would go to Samah. She would know. The fruit vendor, Jonah, was one of the Way. The last he had heard, Samah and her brother Ramoth were staying with him.

Remembering the last time he had seen her, he paused. What if she didn't believe him? What if her reasons for rejecting him were more than his being an unbeliever? After all, he had slain many of her people and helped to destroy the holy city of Jerusalem. There had even been times when he had been unkind to her. She had reason to fear him. Could he convince her otherwise?

He now understood the power of her faith. When you became a believer, it filled your whole being. You wanted only to please the Father who had sent His Son to die alone on a cross. Would she believe that he had actually come to that point in his life?

When he neared the area where Jonah had his block of flats, Sentinel became more alert. Giving a loud *woof*, the dog ran ahead of him. Realizing that he could smell Samah's presence, Cassius smiled.

Cassius climbed the steps to the apartment above. With some reservation, he knocked on the door.

When the door opened, Cassius recognized Jonah's sister. She stared at him in stunned amazement.

"I wish to see Samah."

Her mouth parted in surprise. Cassius was suddenly filled with unease at her look.

"She and Ramoth left for Palestine yesterday."

fourteen

The trip to Palestine took several weeks. First the ship went by way of Alexandria in Egypt, and then backtracked northward through Sinai towards Palestine. Often they were held up by winter storms rocking the sea, and Samah began to despair of ever reaching home.

After landing in Palestine, they would then have a long overland trek through Galilee and into Samaria. Though Samah knew she was free, she found herself constantly looking around her for trouble of some sort.

Ramoth had been quiet most of the voyage, and surprisingly, he had learned to finally quell his reckless personality. When accused of taking another man's spot on the deck of the ship, Ramoth had held his hands out to his sides and told the other man to take it. Samah had been amazed.

The sky was darkening as the sun sank below the horizon. Ramoth found her leaning against the ship's bulwark, her face pressed into the blowing wind.

"I need to ask your forgiveness," he told her quietly.

"For what?" she asked, surprised.

He sighed heavily, turning and facing out towards the ocean. Seagulls dipped and swayed with the wind, a good omen, according to the captain. As the sky darkened with approaching night, they rapidly disappeared from sight.

"How many times did you warn me about spending my time with Ahab and the others? I didn't listen, and for three years you had to suffer because of my stupidity." He assessed her now, noting the rough wool tunic she had purchased before they left Rome. "And then you suffered through months of slavery. . ."

She stopped him with a hand raised to cover his mouth.

"Shhh. It is forgiven."

He pulled her hand away, his expression tense. "You have forgiven me, and I know Jehovah has, also, but I am having a hard time forgiving myself."

Samah smiled. "I have seen a great change in you, my brother. Isn't that what it means to truly repent? You are gentler, more forgiving. I can see that you are honestly trying to turn your life around and make up for past hurts."

He took both of her hands into his. "Samah, if something happens to me and I don't reach Samaria, I want you to promise me that you will go on."

A cold chill passed through her. "Nothing is going to happen to you. Besides, even if it did, then it's likely that something will happen to me, also."

He shook his head. "No, I don't think so. Jehovah has plans for you."

She felt a cloud of doom settle heavily around her. His words had an almost prophetic cadence to them.

"Ramoth. . ."

He placed a finger over her lips. "Just promise me. I want Mother and Father to know that I. . .that I changed."

Staring into his dark brown eyes, she pressed her lips against his finger in a kiss. When he removed his finger, she told him, "I promise."

Satisfied, he nodded. "Now come back to the mat. We need to get some rest before tomorrow."

They settled down among the other passengers. There were few on board since it was winter and traveling was more dangerous. Samah crossed her hands behind her head and stared up at the sky above her. The stars were hidden behind a fast-moving cloud mass.

Her mind refused to relax, and she once again focused on the words Ramoth had said to her. She felt decidedly chilled and not only from the blowing winds. Pulling her blanket around her tightly, she curled on her side into a ball.

Long after she could hear her brother's deep breathing, she

lay awake. If anything did happen to Ramoth, how did he suppose she could make it to Samaria on her own? Even if she could find the way, brigands roamed the hills all through Palestine.

And then her mind wandered into forbidden territory. Images of Cassius attacked her mind with a ruthless disregard for her attempts to thwart them.

Had Trajan been able to convince him of Jehovah's truth? Would he finally be able to lay to rest the demons of his past and move on to a bright future?

Her heart ached with longing. How ironic that Cassius had taken her freedom, given it back, and then taken her heart captive again. As long as it belonged to him, she would never be able to love another. Was this what Jehovah had intended after all?

I have come that they might have life, and have it to the full.

Jesus' words settled into her mind, bringing with it an assurance that her life would be everything the Lord meant for it to be. Someday perhaps Jehovah would see fit to send her another man to love—a gentle man, who loved the Lord with the depth of passion that her own father did.

The rocking of the ship finally lulled her into a dreamless sleep.

In the morning, the clouds had gathered en masse, and the wind began to pick up in velocity. The captain stared with worried eyes at the darkening horizon.

"This doesn't look good," he muttered to no one in particular.

"We should make for land," one of the passengers suggested.

The captain nodded. "Aye, I would do so, but there is nowhere safe along this coast. Our only chance is to try and run ahead enough to reach a safe harbor before the storm hits."

The storm approached quickly, and it soon became apparent that they would not be able to outrun it. The captain gave orders to prepare the ship. The passengers huddled near the main sail, uncertain of what to do.

Samah watched the gathering darkness, offering up prayers

for their safety. Several others had their eyes closed, petitioning whatever deities they worshiped.

Ramoth helped the sailors fasten down amphoras and crates of goods. Samah watched him and felt proud. He had grown in wisdom and caring so much over the last several weeks, and she knew he had finally found a personal savior. She had never seen him look more relaxed, while others scurried around him in fear. His very serenity had others seeking his counsel, even the surly captain.

When the storm finally hit, it hit with breathtaking intensity. The cargo ship lifted on the waves, crashing to the hollows of the sea. Those on deck screamed in fear as they were thrown about like pieces of straw.

Ramoth crawled across the ship to Samah's side, dragging a rope behind him. Tying the rope around her waist, he then fastened it to the mast.

It soon became apparent that the ship would not survive the storm. Passengers and crew alike fought mindlessly for places in the ship's boat that was bobbing on the sea behind the ship.

Ramoth held his sister close. She buried her face into his chest when she saw one man brutally murder another to get his place in the boat.

"I think we'll be safer if we stay with the ship," he yelled above the wind. Then she heard him mumbling and realized that he was praying. She added her prayers to his.

Wind tore at the small aft sail, ripping it from its mooring and flinging it towards them. Samah screamed as she was suddenly engulfed by the fabric. Ramoth helped her fight her way clear, shoving the sail away. It blew across the deck and into the water.

Those who had not made it onto the ship's boat now ran frantically about the deck seeking some means of escape. When the ship fell into a trough, a wave rose on their side, crashing over the deck in a raging tide. The main sail snapped beneath the onslaught.

Moving with the power of the water, Samah was suddenly

lifted from the deck, her waist still tied to the mast. The long wooden arm plunged into the sea. The last thing Samah heard was her brother screaming her name. Her one thought was that it was not Ramoth who would not make it to Samaria, but herself. Lifting her thoughts in one final prayer, she begged Jehovah for Ramoth's life and for his ability to tell their parents just how much she loved them.

&

Cassius stood at the prow of the Roman warship and breathed deeply of the salt air. He willed the ship to go faster, his anxious thoughts with the woman he loved.

It had taken him weeks before he had been able to get a ship to take him to Palestine. None of the cargo ships would sail in the winter, and it was only because more Roman troops were needed at the fortress of Masada that he had been able to finagle this ride.

Sailors scurried up lines and rigging trying to repair the damages after yesterday's storm. The ship had taken a severe pounding, but it had survived the raging tempest.

While the centurion in charge offered a sacrifice to Jupiter, Cassius offered his own thanks for their survival. Frankly, he wouldn't have been surprised had the Almighty chosen to destroy them all. Though his faith in God was growing, he still questioned the reasoning behind the destruction of the Jews.

For centuries, God had cared for His people. Through rebellions and even when they had committed adultery with other gods, He had taken care of them. Why?

Jonah said that it was so that He would have a people to send His Son through. For centuries the Jews had looked for a savior, then when they finally had one, they rejected Him because He didn't live up to their expectations.

Cassius was glad that he had been able to warn Jonah and the others about Vespasian's suspicions. Many were already preparing to leave Rome before a worse persecution than what Nero perpetrated could be instituted.

He prayed for Trajan and his mother. Trajan had decided to marry his mother, surprising both Callista and Cassius. When he had questioned the general, Trajan had told him that he owed it to Callista.

Cassius had reminded him that he didn't love her, but Trajan had told him that love was a decision. He would love her because he had decided to love her.

Shaking his head at such a thought, Cassius couldn't imagine a love affair of the mind. The feelings he had for Samah were intense and filled his very being. He yearned for her in so many ways, not least among them the physical. Her very scent made his blood thunder through his veins.

A soft whine brought his thoughts to an abrupt end. Sentinel lay at his feet, his eyes drooping in misery. Sailing was bad enough, but after yesterday's storm, the dog was truly incapacitated.

Cassius knelt beside him and rubbed his head. "Hang in there, Boy."

He didn't know what to do to help the animal's suffering.

"Captain," a sailor yelled. "There's something off the starboard."

Cassius got to his feet, staring at the floating item in the distance. Scattered debris from a broken vessel bobbed on the sea's swells.

The captain came and stood beside Cassius. "Looks like the poor devils didn't make it."

As they moved closer, they were surrounded by floating casks and crates. All manner of material bobbed on the waves around them.

"Look, Captain! It's a woman!"

Soldiers left their posts to peer at the woman drifting towards them. She was tied to a ship's mast, one arm hanging over it, keeping her from sliding into the water. She didn't move.

"Is she alive?" one soldier shouted.

In the next instant, the post she was attached to turned

and Cassius recognized Samah.

"Samah!"

Throwing off his sandals, he quickly dove into the water. The cold water closed over his head, and he kicked out, surfacing beside the drifting mast. Shaking the water from his head, he pulled himself next to Samah, feeling for a pulse. It beat weakly against his fingertips.

"She's alive!" he yelled up to the captain. "Help me get her aboard."

The crew hurried to do as bid. Dozens of soldiers stood nearby as Samah was lifted to the deck. They helped Cassius into the ship, and pushing out of their detaining hands, he quickly knelt beside Samah, the water dripping from his head.

"You know this woman?" the captain asked.

Cassius nodded, but couldn't speak. He gently pressed the wet hair away from her face. Tracing a path with his finger, he followed the contours of her face across her cheekbones and over her lips.

She stirred, and her eyes fluttered open.

"Cassius?"

Never had Samah seen eyes so tender. "Yes, Beloved. It is I."

She tried to push herself up. "Ramoth!"

Cassius frowned. "He isn't here." He pulled her up until she rested across his lap. "Can you tell us what happened?"

She began to cry. "The storm. And the people went crazy!" She buried her face in her hands. "Oh, Ramoth! Ramoth!"

Cassius looked up at the captain. "See if there are any other survivors."

Though they searched for hours, they found no sign of other survivors or their bodies. Cassius took Samah below into the captain's cabin and laid her on the bunk. Her eyes went past him, and she smiled sadly. Reaching out her hand, she called softly, "It's all right, Sentinel. You can come in."

The dog didn't hesitate. He strutted to her side, whining in agitation.

She stroked his fur, unable to look Cassius in the eyes. He sat down on the bunk beside her. His hungry gaze devoured her.

"I thought I might never see you again," he rasped.

She finally looked him in the eye and was spellbound by the love she saw shining there.

"Thank God, He saved you. I will never cease to sing His praises."

"Did you say *God*?

He smiled then. "God. Jehovah. Whichever name you choose to call Him. Yes, my little Samaritan dove. I have finally found what I have been seeking. The God who has been seeking me." He clutched her hand as though he would never let it go. "Will you marry me now, Beloved? Can you love me, despite what I have done to your people and to you?"

She threw herself into his arms. "I have forgiven you long ago. Oh Cassius, I love you so much!"

He held her tightly, the warmth from his own body mingling with the coolness of hers. He wished that he could hold her like this forever. Reaching behind her, he pulled the blanket from the bunk close and wrapped it around her. She snuggled against the warmth, her teeth chattering with cold.

Sentinel whined, and Samah glanced down at him. Again, she could have sworn that the dog was smiling.

epilogue

Samah and Cassius walked hand in hand up the hill in Sychar. Just beyond the bend lay her parents' house. It had once belonged to her grandfather, but he had left it to his only daughter, her mother.

When they finally entered the courtyard in front of the house, a servant called to someone inside. The door opened slowly, and a woman emerged. Though she was small of stature, she stood straight and proud, her yellow tunic hanging gracefully to her feet. Her graying hair hung in a long braid down her back.

She looked first at the man in the Roman-style garb. Her puzzled expression then turned to the woman at his side. Hazel eyes so like those staring back at her widened in shock.

"Samah!" She stood unmoving, paralyzed with shock. "Dear Jehovah, can it be?"

"Mother." With a cry, Samah threw herself into her mother's arms and wept uncontrollably. Her mother's eyes were lifted upwards, the tears flowing down her cheeks in a river of liquid joy.

"Oh, Jehovah, Jehovah! Thank you for your mercy!"

The door opened wider behind her. A man stepped forth, his frown resting on the Roman and then on the older woman. "Anna? What's going on here?"

Samah lifted her swimming eyes from her mother's breast and stared at him with trembling lips, unable to speak.

"Oh, Barak. Come see what Jehovah has sent home to us."

Barak stood stunned. A small gurgle escaped his throat, and he reached forward, grabbing Samah into his arms.

Cassius stood nearby, glad that Samah had finally been reunited with her family. What amazed him most of all was the fact that Sentinel allowed the exchange. The dog sat at his feet watching the scene serenely, and Cassius could have sworn that there was a grin on the animal's face.

Barak finally turned to Cassius, a question in his eyes. The two men studied each other thoroughly, and Cassius was impressed with the Jew's girth and stature. Though his hair was graying, he was obviously in fine shape.

"Mother, Father, this is Cassius, the man that I wish to marry."

Barak flashed his daughter a look that she had no trouble interpreting. Before Samah could say anything, her mother sent her father a speaking glance. Without words, she could read the messages passing from their eyes.

You were a Jew. I am a Samaritan.

That's different.

How so?

He's a Roman!

Samah ruthlessly interrupted this nonverbal exchange. "Cassius is a child of Christ."

Her mother lifted a delicately shaped eyebrow.

See?

Her father sighed. *All right, I'll give him a chance.*

Reaching out to take Barak's hand for support, Samah told her parents, "There is much I have to tell you. But first, I must tell you of Ramoth."

For the next two hours, Samah sat and cried with her parents over the loss of their only son. She told them of Ramoth's repentance at the end and his prediction of something happening to him.

Cassius sat next to her, uncomfortably aware that he was nothing more than an outsider. He allowed them their time of grief, knowing full well what it was to lose someone you loved.

There was a commotion in the atrium, and a man suddenly burst into the room. He was as tall as Barak, and of similar age and stature. His eyes quickly scanned the perimeter, coming to rest on Samah. They widened in surprise.

"It's true," he breathed slowly. "It's really true."

Samah came to her feet, running and throwing herself into his arms. "Uncle Adonijah!"

A woman followed him, her dark eyes lit with joy. She held out her arms, and Samah went to her. "Oh, Aunt Mara. I thought I would never see you again."

Mara pulled back, her eyes full of tears. She brushed the tendrils of hair back from Samah's face. "Oh, little one. It is so good to see you again."

At the woman's name, Cassius sat forward on his seat. So, this was the woman his Uncle Trajan—correction, his father—had loved for so many years. There was absolutely nothing spectacular about her, unless it would be the huge purple mark on her face.

A young girl about Samah's age pushed her way past Mara. She was petite of frame, her long, dark hair coiled in a rope on her head. She was followed by a young man several years older. Cassius guessed him to be about his own age. Samah reached for both of them at the same time.

"Daniel! Miriam!"

They hugged, everyone laughing and crying at the same time. Finally, Samah turned to Cassius.

"Cassius, this is my family. My Uncle Adonijah, Aunt Mara, and my two cousins, Daniel and Miriam."

Mara looked at Cassius oddly. "Have we met before?" she asked.

"I think not," he denied. He wondered what his blood father would have to say if he could see the woman now. Did she still hold a place in his heart that his mother would never fill? He wondered if he should tell the woman that the seed she had planted so many years ago had borne fruit, but decided that things were better left as they were.

Samah found him some time later standing in the garden watching the sunset. The air grew cold as the sun descended, and Samah shivered.

Cassius pulled her close and wrapped her in his arms, and she snuggled against him, contented. He studied her seriously. "Do you think they will ever accept me?"

She smiled, tracing his lower lip with her finger. The look she gave him was so sultry, it took him by surprise. He could feel the adrenaline rushing through his body in response.

"Of course they will, just as Anticus accepted me."

"You are easy to love," he refuted.

"As are you." Her husky voice twisted his insides.

"How long is a Jewish betrothal?"

She smiled at him coyly. "A year."

He groaned, and she laughed. "Fortunately for you, I do not follow the traditions of my ancestors." She reached up and kissed him lingeringly on the lips. His eyes darkened with emotion. "Ask me sometime," she teased, "about my parents' wedding."

She looked past him and saw a lone figure stumbling up the path that led to the house. Frowning, she wondered who would be coming to her parents' house this late in the evening.

As the figure drew closer, Samah's eyes grew wide, and she shoved herself out of Cassius's arms, running towards what Cassius could make out as the figure of a man.

Cassius heard Samah yell and saw the man grab for her. Terror and wrath gripped him so hard he could hardly breathe. Running, he pulled up short when he saw Samah crying in her brother's arms. Tired and bedraggled, Ramoth grinned at him.

"I thought I might see you again."

At Samah's yell, the others rushed from the house. Sheer pandemonium broke out when they recognized Ramoth, and Cassius stood nearby smiling as he watched the whole scene play out over again. Holding his weeping mother close, Ramoth explained his delivery from the watery grave that had claimed so many of the people on the ship.

The joy of the reunited family warmed Cassius's heart. When the others went inside, Samah returned to his side. She took his hand and stared at him with starry eyes filled with love.

"If not for you, Ramoth would not have found his own personal relationship with the Lord. He has always leaned on our parents' faith, but it never satisfied. That's why he was always so impetuous. He was looking for something and didn't know where to find it."

Cassius looked doubtful.

"It's true. The apostle Paul said that all things work together for the good of those who love the Lord. Everything that has happened has been to fulfill Jehovah's own plan."

She came into his arms again. "Oh, Cassius, don't you see? Everything led us to each other, and you to the Lord. I don't begrudge a single day, a single minute. I would do it all over again in a heartbeat."

Cassius pulled her close, lowering his mouth to hers. Their kiss lingered, pulling them ever closer to each other until their hearts sang as one. At last, Cassius had come home.

Miriam cleared her throat, and they parted reluctantly. Samah's cousin dimpled beguilingly at Cassius. At least one member of Samah's family had no trouble accepting him.

"Father wanted me to tell you that your dog is missing," she told them, never taking her eyes from Cassius.

Startled, both Samah and Cassius pushed past her and hurried inside. Though they searched for some time, they could find no sign of the animal. Cassius's whistle pierced the night air over and over, but there was no response. Disheartened, they finally gave up.

"He went just as he came," Cassius told her, and she could hear the hurt in his voice.

"Perhaps his job is finished," she answered, her own heart breaking at thought of losing the dog. How mysterious that the animal should come and go in such a way.

Slowly they returned to the villa, aching for their loss, yet consoled in each other's love.

Far off in the distance, a lonely howl rose to the night sky.

A Letter To Our Readers

Dear Reader:

In order that we might better contribute to your reading enjoyment, we would appreciate your taking a few minutes to respond to the following questions. We welcome your comments and read each form and letter we receive. When completed, please return to the following:

Rebecca Germany, Fiction Editor
Heartsong Presents
PO Box 719
Uhrichsville, Ohio 44683

1. Did you enjoy reading *Captive Heart* by Darlene Mindrup?
   ☐ Very much! I would like to see more books
   by this author!
   ☐ Moderately. I would have enjoyed it more if

   _____

   _____

   _____

2. Are you a member of **Heartsong Presents**? Yes ☐ No ☐
   If no, where did you purchase this book?_____

   _____

3. How would you rate, on a scale from 1 (poor) to 5 (superior), the cover design?_____

4. On a scale from 1 (poor) to 10 (superior), please rate the following elements.

   _____ Heroine   _____ Plot

   _____ Hero   _____ Inspirational theme

   _____ Setting   _____ Secondary characters

5. These characters were special because_____

_____

_____

6. How has this book inspired your life?_____

_____

_____

7. What settings would you like to see covered in future
   Heartsong Presents books?_____

_____

_____

8. What are some inspirational themes you would like to see
   treated in future books?_____

_____

_____

9. Would you be interested in reading other **Heartsong
   Presents** titles?   Yes ❏   No ❏

10. Please check your age range:
    ❏ Under 18   ❏ 18-24   ❏ 25-34
    ❏ 35-45   ❏ 46-55   ❏ Over 55

11. How many hours per week do you read? _____

Name _____

Occupation _____

Address _____

City _____ State _____ Zip _____

OREGON

*I*n the majestic Pacific Northwest of the early twentieth century, the Galloway siblings attempt to make their mark on the world—and, perhaps, find life partners to join them on the way.

A new century has dawned with its marvels of modernization that promise to change the world. But amidst all that's new, the unchanging nature of love—and of God—remains. You'll be charmed by the inspirational love stories of *Oregon*.

paperback, 464 pages, 5 ³⁄₁₆" x 8"

····Hearts♥ng····

DARLENE MINDRUP is a full-time homemaker and homeschool teacher. A "radical feminist" turned "radical Christian," Darlene lives in Arizona with her husband and two children. She believes "romance is for everyone, not just the young and beautiful."

Books by Darlene Mindrup

HEARTSONG PRESENTS
HP207—The Eagle and the Lamb
HP224—Edge of Destiny
HP243—The Rising Son
HP280—A Light Within
HP315—My Enemy, My Love
HP336—Drink from the Sky
HP376—Mark of Cain

Don't miss out on any of our super romances. Write to us at the following address for information on our newest releases and club information.

Heartsong Presents Readers' Service
PO Box 719
Uhrichsville, OH 44683

The intensity of his look unnerved Samah.

She had never been reticent about sharing her story with anyone, but the fact that the man across from her represented all the power of Rome made her hesitate. Romans hated Christians, of that she was certain. But perhaps it was for this very reason that Jehovah had brought her to this position. She would be careful with what she said, but she would be honest.

"I'm a Christian, Tribune."

His eyes widened in amazement. He said nothing for some time, and Samah could see him trying to digest what she had revealed and how it would affect him.

"I'm surprised that you would admit it," he told her finally. "Surely you know that that religion has been forbidden by the emperor."

Samah smiled slightly. "Which emperor? I know of Nero, but I have heard nothing of Vespasian's thoughts on the matter."

"Then let me apprize you of his feelings," he told her dryly. "Should you happen to mention it to him he will most likely have you burned, if not crucified."

She opened her mouth, but the words dried up in her throat when he reached across the space between them, cupping her chin in his palm. His eyes were dark with anger.

"You will say nothing of this to anyone; do I make myself clear?"

Although she knew that the apostle Paul had said that one must obey one's master, she also knew that he had said to obey God above all else. She finally managed to push the words out of her mouth.

"I will not lie."

She saw his eyes darken further. "You will if I command you to."

It took every ounce of strength she possessed to shake her head negatively. She was more than a little frightened by his rigid stance. His nostrils flared outwards, and he released her.

"If you are foolish enough to admit to such a religion, I will not protect you."